I0650299

Susie Frances Harrison

Pine, Rose and Fleur de Lis

Susie Frances Harrison

Pine, Rose and Fleur de Lis

ISBN/EAN: 9783337415471

Printed in Europe, USA, Canada, Australia, Japan

Cover: Foto ©Andreas Hilbeck / pixelio.de

More available books at **www.hansebooks.com**

PINE, ROSE

—AND—

FLEUR DE LIS

—BY—

S. FRANCES HARRISON

(SERANUS)

Author of "Crowded Out and other Sketches"
The "Canadian Birthday Book," etc.

TORONTO
HART & COMPANY
31 & 33 KING ST. WEST
1891

CONTENTS.

DOWN THE RIVER.

THE FRIEND.

Was it at a dinner, glum,
Was it at a kettledrum?
Was it at the rink, the play,
Where was it, O friend, I pray—
First we talked of schemes like these,
Longed to taste the eastern breeze,
Longed to go away together
In a flash of summer weather,
Where the Gallic pulses beat
Quickly in the quiet street;
Where a quainter life prevails,
And no modern strife assails;
Where few others seldom go,
Where the red-doored houses low
Stand behind the stately row
Of leafy poplars, where they show
Famous hollyhocks and vines,
Where they make their own sweet wines,

Chat and weave and spin and knit
All the day—O picture it !
Where there flames the marigold
Side by side with sunflowers bold,
And the Norman asters hold
Colloquy with columbine,
Aquilegia—spurred and fine,
Canadensis—yellow-red,
Stem erect and drooping head—
Where the gabled houses meet
Almost o'er the grass-grown street,
Where the maidens kneel and pray
At the Cross beside the way,
While their mothers rake the hay.

That is—so my friends all say—
How they live at Côte Beaupré,
That is where we two shall go,
Hear them talk or watch them sew,
Help them, shall we—once to sing
Gai le rosier—that pretty thing—
Pimpanipole and Claire Fontaine,
And many another haunting strain?
How they'll laugh and how they'll stare,
When they hear us hum the air
Of *St. Malo,* and *Guignoleé,*
V'la bon vent, and *P'tit Bonnet !*

Well, well, well, I see it all ;
Presbytère and poplars tall,
Wayside Cross and lichen'd wall,
Dark-eyed *gamin* brown and fat,

Cheerful *curé* fond of chat,
Sparkling spires among the hills,
Water falls and roadside rills,
Blueberries in birch canoes
Brought by boys in wooden shoes,
Cones of berries red and sweet
Brought by girls in bare brown feet,
And behind it all, the pride
Of the lofty Laurentide
Mountain range so misty blue,
All the glorious, peerless view
Of the river flowing down
Past Cape Diamond's jewell'd crown;
Past each sleepy little town
White against the hillside brown,
Past Ste. Anne's where you may see
Relics of a fealty
Long since dead in wiser places,
Plann'd by cautious, colder races;
Past the Isle of Bacchus, where
All the past is in the air,
And in song and shoe we deem
La belle France to be supreme.

Past Tourmente we then shall float
In our yellow open boat,
All along the spar-bright shore
Lightly land and swift explore,
While the garnet-threaded cliff
Hangs above our yellow skiff,
And the eyeless fossils wait
Friendly hammer in their slate.

Eurypterus remipes—he
Is the one we long to see,
But I fear he did not grow
Quite so very far below.
Simple types, content us then;
Fossils fit to match the men;
We decline our souls to vex
With a type at all complex;
Graptolites will do for us,
Asaphus platycephalus,
Or *Trinocleus concentricus.*
As to flora—why, they say,
Nowhere are the woods so gay
As around fair Murray Bay.
Beds of Cornus red as wax,
Blossoms blue as azure flax,
Yards and yards of rosy bells,
Sweet Linnæa—deck the dells,
Carpet all the forest floor,
And the terraced land is crown'd,
Every hill and every mound,
With a grass as purely green
As in England e'er was seen.
All the country round about
Set with streams of perch and trout,
Crystal clear as streams should be
In this land so fair and free.
'Tis no dream, no fallacy.
He, my brother, Crémazie,
Saw it all as we shall see,
That is, if you go with me.
This dear landscape meant for him

DOWN THE RIVER.

More than grey cathedral dim,
Steeped in incense, sweet with chime
In the mellow evening time;
More than ancient parapet,
Storied mosque and minaret,
Much, much more than palace halls
Crumbling under Moorish walls.
What to him were Cadiz, Venice,
Pisa, Paris, Florence, Rome,
All the world beyond the foam?
These he measured without menace
At their value, then his heart
Without seeming, without art,
Craved for Canada, for home.

When the sunrise wakes the pines,
When the saffron glory shines
On the stirring of the loon,
On the sleepy, pallid moon,
When the wood awakes to shiver
In the cool breath of the river,
Flowing, blowing, flowing down
Past Cape Diamond's jewell'd crown,
And the spray that wets the lips,
As we float among the ships,
Holds a precious grain of salt—
Gracious gift and darling fault—
Then the sternest must confess
To the perfect loveliness
Of this province old and quaint,
Sans utilitarian taint.

And when sunset spreads its fires
Over all the slender spires,
When the long Laurentians blue
(O the glorious peerless view!)
Take the amethystine hue
Of a summer evening sky,
Late in June or through July,
Or perhaps in late September,
You will all your life remember,
Spells of Nature's magic weaving,
Almost past our mild believing,
While the vesper bells resound,
Dear to people darkly bound,
(So say those who strain and strive
These same happy ones to drive
Far from ancient goal and gyve),
And the crimson vapours fly,
Leaving orange ones on high.
Last, the amber pales to green,
And o'er all the charmèd scene
Deep the veil of dusk is drawn.
*   *   *   *   *   *

Thus the beauty of the dawn,
Thus the beauty of the night,
Shall encompass with delight
You and me as close we sit
In our boat—O, picture it!

THE FLIGHT.

But enough! Come! Let us go
　　To these charmèd hills and plains,
Far from flat Ontario.

Far from ills that towns bestow,
　　Far from stocks and shares and drains—
But enough! Come! Let us go!

We are tired of style and show,
　　Longing for the fresh campaigns,
Far from flat Ontario,

Where the rushing rapids flow,
　　Where the green hill-side enchains—
But enough! Come! Let us go!

Say good-bye to all you know!
　　We are bound for new domains,
Far from flat Ontario.

All the way we mean to row,
　　You and I, despising trains—
But enough! Come! Let us go
Far from flat Ontario.

AFLOAT AT LAST.

Afloat—we cry—afloat at last!
    Still the city we descry!
While our city hearts beat fast!

Tower and steeple, wharf and mast,
    Black they look but quick they fly,
Afloat—we cry—afloat at last!

Blowing up, a freshening blast
    Ruffles all the lake and sky,
While our city hearts beat fast,

And with one look backward cast,
    All our oars we trembling try,
Afloat—we cry—afloat at last!

Joy! The city's nearly passed,
    Smoke, and dust and din, good-bye!
While our city hearts beat fast.

Pull, my friend! Ahoy! Avast!
    Speech with service should comply,
Afloat—we cry—afloat at last,
While our city hearts beat fast!

THE HOPE.

This, my friend, shall be our part
　　In this summer scheme of ours,
Just to grow a summer heart,

Leaving ways of mire and mart,
　　Octopus, that peace devours,
This, my friend, shall be our part.

Shall we then by nature's art,
　　Try 'mid fields and flocks and flowers
Just to grow a summer heart?

Leave all answers cold and tart,
　　All the city temper sours,
This, my friend, shall be our part,

Make a fresh and honest start,
　　Strive through long and lovely hours
Just to grow a summer heart;

Fear to hurt and fear to thwart,
　　Clearer sense of mighty Powers—
This, my friend, shall be our part,
Just to grow a summer heart.

NOCTURNE.

O Summer on the lake is fair,
    Yet chilly when the sun has fled,
Yet damp where clings the cool night air!

Wrapped in our cloaks we sit just where
    We'll watch the moon her measure tread,
O Summer on the lake is fair!

In town the people in despair
    Bewail the heat in torment dread.
Though damp where clings the cool night air,

We do not fear its breath to share,
    Nor dream of such a thing as bed—
O Summer on the lake is fair!

The breeze it blows about the hair,
    The boat is warm with wraps o'erspread,
Yet damp where clings the cool night air;

To Heaven there winds a starry stair,
    A diamond world is overhead—
O Summer on the lake is fair,
Yet damp where clings the cool night air!

VIGIL.

Shall we sit here and watch the dawn,
    Fair Eos, mother rosy pale,
Or did I catch the faintest yawn?

Base knight that holdest sleep in pawn,
    And would'st not wake to see the Grail,
Shall we sit here and watch the dawn?

Upon me dost thou dare to fawn,
    In vigil vow thou did'st not quail—
Or did I catch the faintest yawn?

The foam is fair as whitest lawn,   .
    The moonbeams leave a silver trail,
Shall we sit here and watch the dawn?·

Or like the fashionable spawn,
    Deem lonely skies of no avail—
Did I not catch the faintest yawn?

Soon will the moon have soft withdrawn,
    E'en now the stars begin to fail,
Shall we sit here and watch the dawn,
Or did I catch the faintest yawn?

THEOCRITUS.

Lives there none other I would see
    Within this boat along with us,
'Tis perfect now with you and me.

Pagan, Protestant, bond or free—
    Unless it were Theocritus—
Lives there none other I would see,

And he is dead—it may not be—
    Yet he had not been frivolous—
'Tis perfect now with you and me.

He had enjoyed it much, had he,
    And envied us our exodus.
Lives there none other I would see,

Making the doubtful number three,
    Proving, perhaps, an incubus—
'Tis perfect now with you and me.

The " Singer of Persephone "—
    He might have loved to voyage thus,
Lives there none other I would see,
'Tis perfect now with you and me.

THEOCRITUS.

Theocritus had kept awake,
    Taken some vivifying dose,
And lost his sleep for summer's sake.

Happy with me thus to partake
    The glories of the scene globose,
Theocritus had kept awake,

And dropped his voice and feared to make
    Remarks and *jeu des mots* jocose,
And lost his sleep for summer's sake.

Your knightly promises you break ;
    By turns you're sleepy, tired, morose,
Theocritus had kept awake.

But me, there's no one on the lake
    Has cared to come to nature close,
And lost his sleep for summer's sake.

I'll have to try a gentle shake—
    How can you be so very gross ?
Theocritus had kept awake
And lost his sleep for summer's sake.

PARANTHESE.

No Dryad in the oak,
   No Nymph within the valley,
No fairy little folk
   To frolic, dance and dally;

No Pan along the shore,
   No Nereid in the water,
No savage shape of boar,
   No fair Demeter's daughter;

No Satyr in the vine,
   No Faun anear the fountain,
No magic in the mine,
   No myth upon the mountain;

No honey amber clear,
   No gleam of waxen laurel,
No stags beside the mere,
   No high Olympic quarrel;

No breath of lowing herds,
   No pastoral sweet singing,
No dish of snow-white curds,
   No mellow milk-bells ringing;

No Goddesses at all,
　　No Gods, or hardly any,
No shapes that might recall,
　　The classic miscellany ;

Dramatis personæ,
　　Theocritus, were wanting,
Save that perchance to thee,
　　Would prove as surely haunting,

The sumach fringèd cliff,
　　The oriole low flying,
The open yellow skiff,
　　The languid loon's far crying,

The resinous keen breeze,
　　The water's lazy lapping,
The silver coated trees,
　　The eagle's idle flapping.

THE THOUSAND ISLANDS.

We are tired of the tumult and turmoil of water
    around us,
Our boat would we bear to a bright and a blossoming
    shore,
The Islands appear and as longing for land they have
    found us.

And their beauty of birch and their selvedge of shadow
    hath bound us
In bonds that bewitch as we blindly approach and adore—
We are tired of the tumult and turmoil of water around us,

And are fain to forget all the winds that have sear'd
    and embrown'd us,
All we pray for—to land, but to enter, escape, we implore,
The Islands appear and as longing for land they have
    found us.

Like Odysseus the deep that for days upon days darkly
    wound us
Becomes but a bane and a blight in its breadth evermore,
We are tired of the tumult and turmoil of water around us.

Bid farewell to the Lake for its fetterless floods have
    nigh drown'd us,
Like the sea can it smite, like the ocean can rage and
    can roar,
The Islands appear and as longing for land they have
    found us.

Like Odysseus again do we dream of delights that once
    crown'd us,
We straight would slip sheer to the grass and give over
    the oar,
We are tired of the tumult and turmoil of water around us,
The Islands appear and as longing for land they have
    found us.

INTERIM.

We must have lain here for an hour or more,
    With a birch above for a ceiling—
We were both so glad to get ashore!

We sang as the skiff we rockward bore,
    With the eagle aloft and wheeling!
We must have lain here for an hour or more,

Learning again the sweet land lore,
    With the air so warm and healing!
We were both so glad to get ashore.

Watching the cumuli slowly soar,
    All the blue beneath revealing,
We must have lain here for an hour or more.

Brown pine tassels bestrew the floor,
    With the red birch fit for peeling!
We were both so glad to get ashore.

The summer's heart is ripe to the core,
    With our own hearts madly reeling!
We must have lain here for an hour or more,
We were both so glad to get ashore!

EXTREMES.

Man's never satisfied, is it not plain!
  Here are we, tired of the endless rowing,
Pleased to be pressing the grasses again!

How many days since one heard the refrain—
  " Life upon land is the poorest thing going!"
Man's never satisfied, is it not plain?

Trite though the proverb, 'tis true in the main;
  Here we are freed from the torrent's flowing,
Pleased to be pressing the grasses again.

Winter or summer, or sunshine or rain,
  Skies that are sunny or skies that are snowing,
Man's never satisfied, is it not plain?

Dear is the river, yet dearer the twain,
  Forest and field, where we watch the trees blowing,
Pleased to be pressing the grasses again.

What we aspire to and what we attain,
  Different—very—by their own showing.
Man's never satisfied; we're—it is plain—
Pleased to be pressing the grasses again!!

RHAPSODIE. (1)

Like a castle of old lies our island—our island so
    greenly extended,
The river runs round it and makes itself like to a moat,
Our island's our castle, so safe—so safe and so simply
    defended.

One side is carved round in the rock, like a branch, like
    a bow that is bended,
Its hollow a haven wherein we have anchor'd the boat,
Like a castle of old lies our island—our island so greenly
    extended.

The other side shelving by steps that no feet but our
    own e'er descended,
Leads down to a bath of clear amber as high as the
    throat,
Our island's our castle, so safe,—so safe and so simply
    defended.

The odd-pinnate leaves of the sumach, our pennons, our
    banners suspended,
Burn scarlet-serrate on the air as they flash and they
    float,
Like a castle of old lies our island—our island so greenly
    extended.

Down always the drawbridge of stones—gray stones with
brown beach ever blended,
Ever up the portcullis that hanging pine fringes denote,
Our island's our castle, so safe—so safe and so simply
defended.

To guard its sweet growth and to cherish its charms to
our hearts thus commended,
Our souls for the space of a night and a day we devote;
Like a castle of old lies our island—our island so greenly
extended,
Our island's our castle, so safe—so safe and so simply
defended.

RHAPSODIE. (II)

Ring'd round with the dark green St. Laurent our isle
    as a jewel is set,
Moss'd agate in emerald rimm'd with an amethyst rare,
One link in the leafy green chain, one star in the stone
    coronet,

That crowns and encircles the brow of the peerless and
    proud rivulet,
A diadem Deity-plac'd—and a mortal's despair!
Ring'd round with the dark green St. Laurent our isle
    as a jewel is set,

While glowing with feverish garnet, its sands sparkle
    bright in the wet,
And clear as Brazilian topaz its summits declare
One link in the leafy green chain, one star in the stone
    coronet.

The lichen upon it is writing in God's orange own
    alphabet,
And dimly we measure its message, while past all compare
Ring'd round with the dark green St. Laurent our isle
    as a jewel is set.

And here as we stand on its summit, glad warders on
    grey parapet,
A thousand such jewels are sparkling in midsummer air ;
One link in the leafy green chain, one star in the stone
    coronet,

One gem, and but one—of a thousand—is this whereon
    rest has been met,
And dimly we worship its beauty, while shining and fair,
Ring'd round with the dark green St. Laurent our isle
    as a jewel is set,
One link in the leafy green chain, one star in the stone
    coronet.

EN AVANT!

We must be off, my mutineer,
    The limpid wave to splash and skim,
To-day you are requir'd to steer.

The wind is fair, nor yet doth veer,
    'Tis five—by all the cherubim!
We must be off, my mutineer.

No more, O lazy sonneteer,
    Of verses wrought in idle whim,
To-day you are requir'd to steer.

The sun is high and chanticleer
    On land doth raise his morning hymn,
We must be off, my mutineer!

Now for a day without compeer,
    The long, long row, the cooling swim.
To-day you are requir'd to steer

Silent as fish and swift as deer
    Among these isles. Sit down and trim !
We must be off, my mutineer;
To-day you are requir'd to steer.

FAIRY DOCKS.

Beautiful, these lichen'd rocks,
    Russet vein'd and amber plated,
Fit for fragile fairy docks;

Red-brown, like the furry fox,
    Orange til'd and silver slated—
Beautiful, these lichen'd rocks!

Beautiful, their arching blocks,
    Purple scarr'd and white striated,
Fit for fragile fairy docks.

Bronze, the ruffled mat that mocks
    At our wit, how propagated—
Beautiful, these lichen'd rocks!

Steer us through them, linkèd locks,
    Gold and green illuminated,
Fit for fragile fairy docks!

Fairy shallops! Fear no shocks!
    Float secure! For you created,
Beautiful, these lichen'd rocks,
Fit for fragile fairy docks.

ROUND THE FIRE.

The pipe, the book, the blazing fire,
The cheap yet dear delights of camp,
Of these we never, never tire.

We rise at four—duty, desire,
Are one, so nobly off we tramp,
—The pipe, the book, the blazing fire

To earn —unmoor the boat, acquire
The fish that bear Ontario's stamp,
Of these we never, never tire.

At six we're back. The sun climbs higher,
We crave the evening, cool and damp,
The pipe, the book, the blazing fire.

The hot hours pass 'mid bud and briar;
The wildwood fruits we choose and champ,
Of these we never, never tire.

Till after dusk these three conspire,
(When one in town doth light her lamp)
The pipe, the book, the blazing fire—
Of these we never, never tire.

LOATH TO GO.

So we linger, loath to leave
(Stretched upon a bracken bed)
Such an island, such an eve!

Still unto the waters cleave
Sunset yellows, pink and red,
While we linger, loath to leave,

Fearing fate no more may weave
Plot so fair as that which bred
Such an island, such an eve.

Still the languid waters heave
Purpled and encarmined,
So we linger, loath to leave.

Twilight gray doth not bereave
Earth of beauty. Ne'er were wed
Such an island, such an eve!

Yet we must press on, achieve,
Cease to dream, and do instead—
Still we linger, loath to leave
Such an island, such an eve!

ENTR'ACTE.

Yes; we linger, though we know
   Fairer scenes await below,
Fairer to our western eyes
Through the medium of surprise
Than perhaps they really show,
Yet we linger, loath to go.
We would not be held ingrate,
Nor a tithe of love abate
For the blue Adagio
Of our own Ontario;
We would not be sycophant,
Changeable and complaisant,
Never would we seek to raise
Just a mount of paraphrase,
Rant and rhetoric, and varnish
Thick with flattery, then garnish
All with jewelled gauds and tropes,
(Gems that very quickly tarnish)
Frantic flights and hectic hopes.

Though, I say, I do not seek
That my rhyming should bespeak
Overpraise for that sweet strip,
Strip of sparkling shores that dip
In St. Laurent's hallowed wave—
And although I do not hold
That my native air is cold,
Wholly damp and destitute
Of the kind of warmer fruit
All my soul doth warmly crave,
Still the blue Adagio
And the placid boundless flow
Of my own Ontario
Doth oppress me, doth not please,
As the lesser royalties,
Livelier currents, tawny, brown,
Lucent, shimmering, flowing down
Past each spire-deckt little town.

Thus to you I fain would show
First the foaming Gatineau;
And the wild *prestissimo*
Of its snowy cascades, set
Round about with violet
Shadows cast by mighty pines;
All the hues that dawn divines
In the rolling lumber, wet,
Sun-fired jasper, glassy jet.
Yes! these pulsing currents run
Swifter, subtler, while they shun
Travelled paths and common gaze,
Following shyer, sweeter ways.

This is where we next shall go—
Up the gleaming Gatineau.
Leap—the heart, and flash—the eye!
Let who will go on, pass by—
We at least have come to stay
—Where the *habitant* hath sway!
So—away!

OTTAWA.

I.

Three are the cliffs, and three the winding rivers,
High on the cliffs' crest risèth the crownèd town;
    Three are the cliffs, and one the Fall with its thunder
    Shaking the bridge while the river rolleth under,
Flicking the wild white foam from its lips so brown.

II.

A city set on a hill may not be hidden,
Her sunlit towers from afar transcend the green;
    Three are her hills, as an Old World town's were
        seven,
    And from all three her spires ascend to heaven,
Like nests in the cliff her homes in the rock are seen.

III.

Fair is the view when the morning mists are melting,
Bridge and river and tree awake in the dark;
    Fairer yet when the rosy clouds of vesper
    Fire all the Gothic glass, and fair when Hesper
Shoots at the blue his tiny silvery mark.

IV.

But fairest of all when the winter sun is glowing,
And the bluest sky in the world is overhead,
    Or when at night all the jewell'd lights are shining,
    And the twisted ribbons of fire are gaily twining
Around her pines to the sound of her children's tread.

V.

*Outaouai!   Whatever else betide her,
Beauty is hers for a birthright sure and sweet,
    And old Romance, could he see her rocks and ridges,
    Could he stand but once on her spray-swept stormy
        bridges,
Would grow young again as he cast himself at her feet.

* Original Indian.

GATINEAU POINT.

A half-breed, slim, and sallow of face,
    Alphonse lies full length on his raft,
The hardy son of a hybrid race.

Lithe and long, with the Indian grace,
    Vers'd in the varied Indian craft,
A half-breed, slim, and sallow of face,

He nurses within mad currents that chase—
    The swift, the sluggish—a foreign graft,
This hardy son of a hybrid race.

What southern airs, what snows embrace
    Within his breast—soft airs that waft
The half-breed—slim, and sallow of face,

Far from the Gatineau's foaming base!
    And what strong potion hath he quaff'd,
This hardy son of a hybrid race,

That upon this sun-bak'd blister'd place
    He sleeps, with his hand on the burning haft,
A Metis—slim, and sallow of face,
The hardy son of a hybrid race!

THE VOYAGEUR.

Like the swarthy son of some tropic shore
    He sleeps, with his olive bosom bar'd,
He sleeps—in his earrings of brassy ore.

Like a tawny tiger whom hot hours bore,
    When all night long he has growled and glar'd
At the swarthy son of some tropic shore,

Like a fierce-ey'd blossom with heart of gore
    That too long in the sun-flush'd fields has flar'd,
He sleeps—in his earrings of brassy ore,

And his scarlet sash that he gaily wore
    To tempt Madelon—who his heart has snar'd,
Like the swarthy son of some tropic shore.

That dusky form might a queen adore—
    Prenez garde, Madelon, for a season spar'd,
He sleeps—in his earrings of brassy ore.

For a season only. What may be in store
    For Madelon? She who has never car'd!
    *   *   *   *   *   *   *

Like the swarthy son of some tropic shore
He sleeps—in his earrings of brassy ore.

DANGER.

Well! Let him sleep! Time enough to awake
    When sunset ushers a kind release,
When cooling shadows the raft overtake.

For Madelon's heart will never break
    For Alphonse, but for Verrier, *fils,*
So—let him sleep. Time enough to awake

When Verrier, dressed for Madelon's sake
    In his best, is up the river a piece,
When cooling shadows the raft overtake.

A Carmen—she – whose eyelashes make
    Havoc with all—old Boucher's niece—
So! Let him sleep, time enough to awake,

For a desperate thing is a bad heart-ache,
    And one that may not entirely cease
When cooling shadows the raft overtake.

If they met, who knows—a spring, a shake,
    A jack-knife, deadly as Malay creece—
Hush! Let him sleep! Time enough to awake
When cooling shadows the raft overtake.

LES CHANTIERS.

For know, my girl, there is always the axe
      Ready at hand in this latitude,
And how it stings and bites and hacks

When Alphonse the sturdy trees attacks!
      So fear, child, to cross him, or play the prude,
For know, my girl, there is always the axe.

See! it shines even now as his hands relax
      Their grip with a dread desire imbu'd,
And how it stings and bites and hacks,

And how it rips and cuts and cracks
      —Perhaps—in his brain as the foe is pursu'd,
For know, my girl, there is always the axe.

The giant boles in the forest tracks
      Stagger, soul-smitten, when afar it is view'd,
And how it stings and bites and hacks!

Then how, Madelon, should its fearful thwacks
      A slender lad like your own elude?
For know, my girl, there is always the axe,
And how it stings! and bites! and hacks!

CHATEAU PAPINEAU.

(Afloat.)

I.

The red til'd towers of the old Château
　　Perch'd on the cliff above our bark,
Burn in the western evening glow.

The fiery spirit of Papineau
　　Consumes them still with its fever spark,
The red til'd towers of the old Château!

Drift by and mark how bright they show,
　　And how the mullion'd windows—mark!
Burn in the western evening glow!

Drift down, or up, where'er you go,
　　They flame from out the distant park,
The red til'd towers of the old Château.

So was it once with friend, with foe;
　　Far off they saw the patriot's ark
Burn in the western evening glow.

Think of him now! One thought bestow,
　　As, blazing against the pine trees dark,
The red til'd towers of the old Château
Burn in the western evening glow!

(Ashore)

II.

Within this charmèd cool retreat
    Where bounty dwelt and beauty waits,
The Old World and the New World meet.

Quitting the straggling village street,
    Enter,—passing the great gray gates,
Within this charmèd cool retreat.

Where thrives a garden, ancient, neat,
    Where vulgar noise ne'er penetrates,
The Old World and the New World meet.

For mouldering vault and carven seat
    Tell us that France predominates
Within this charmèd cool retreat,

Though Canada be felt in beat
    Of summer pulse that enervates.
The Old World and the New World meet

In dial, arbour, tropic heat.
    Enter! And note, how clear all states—
That in this charmèd cool retreat,
The Old World and the New World meet.

III.

The garden's past. 'Tis forest now
    Encircling us with leafy tide,
Close clustering in green branch and bough.

So beautiful a wood, we vow,
    Was never seen, so fresh, so wide.
The garden's past, 'tis forest now,

'Tis more, 'tis Canada, and how
    Should feudal leaven lurk and hide
Close clustering in green branch and bough?

Quaintly the dial on the brow
    Of yonder open glade is spied;
The garden's past, 'tis forest now,

Yet doth the dial straight endow
    The green with glamour undenied,
Close clustering in green branch and bough.

Such relics who would disallow?
    We pause and ponder; turn aside;
The garden's past, 'tis forest now,
Close clustering in green branch and bough.

IV.

The glint of steel, the gleam of brocade,
   "Monseigneur" up in his tarnish'd frame,
A long low terrace, half sun, half shade;

Tapestry, dusty, dim and fray'd,
   Fauteuil and sofa, a flickering flame,
A glint of steel, a gleam of brocade;

"Mdme" on the wall as a roguish maid,
   Later—some years—as a portly dame,
The long low terrace, half sun, half shade,

Where "Mdme's" ghost and "Monsieur's" parade,
   And play at *ombre,* their favorite game!
The glint of steel, the gleam of brocade

Hang over hall and balustrade.
   Paceth a spectral peacock tame
The long low terrace, half sun, half shade.

Waketh a nightly serenade
   Where daylight now we see proclaim
The glint of steel, the gleam of brocade,
The long low terrace, half sun, half shade!

V.

The spell of Age is over all,
The lichen'd vault, the massive keep,
The shaded walks, the shadowy hall,

And mediæval mists enthral
The senses bath'd in beauty sleep,
The spell of age is over all!

No marvel if a silken shawl
Be sometimes heard to trail and sweep
The shaded walks, the shadowy hall.

No marvel if a light footfall
Adown the stair be heard to creep—
The spell of age is over all.

A foot—we muse—both arch'd and small,
Doth often tread this terrace steep,
Those shaded walks, this shadowy hall,

A foot as white as trilliums tall—
Musing, the wall we lightly leap.
The spell of Age is over all!
The shaded walks—the shadowy hall.

ENTR' ACTE.

I kept my promises, you see,
I show'd you barge and crowded quay.

I show'd you swarthy, sunburnt faces,
Born of the mix'd and alien races.

I show'd you how the tropic noon
Enwraps the raft in heavy swoon,

And how the story old is found
Upon this new and northern ground.

I show'd you how the solemn crowd
Within the great Cathedral bow'd.

And once together we have view'd
A genuine Gallic market feud.

The tall Basilica has lifted
High towers above where we have drifted.

Its golden cross has far to shine;
For all the valley 'tis the sign,

For all the Pèche, the Pickanoe,
And all the gleaming Gatineau.

O how leapt our spirits up,
(Like the crystal in the cup.)

When at Thurso first we heard
Natalie, our contralto bird,

Shy and slim, brown-ey'd, fifteen,
With her fearless walk and mien,

And her songs of twenty verses,
Songs once sung by Norman nurses!

Long we lay and listen'd, lying,
Trusty oars no longer plying,

Stretch'd beneath the sumach's shade,
While the fearless dark-ey'd maid

Sang of castles, cavaliers,
Perils, patches, kisses, tears,

And the intervals so tender
Made our sordid souls surrender

To a modern "nutt browne mayde,"
Darkest hair in heaviest braid,

Darkest eyes and olive cheek,
Eyes both mischievous and meek:

Do thou not, my friend, forget
Dainty featur'd Nicolette,

Aucassin, her lover bold—
All the dainty story, told

In the antique measur'd verse,
Quaint *tirade* and metre terse.

*   *   *   *   *

So when danger threaten'd, we
Bade farewell to Natalie,

Bade farewell to island, shore,
Open roof and forest floor,
Languidly upheld the oar.

AT. STE. THERESE.

I.

The quaint stiff metres of olden France !
Strange, to hear them in Ste. Thérèse,
Metres that speak of duel and dance,

Of gay parterre and of trim pleasance, .
Of swords that flash and fringe that frays—
The quaint stiff metres of olden France !

In his sash and *tuque* with his keen gay glance,
Hark to Maxime as he lustily brays
Metres that speak of duel and dance,

Measures that ring with old-world romance,
Ballads, rondels, and virelays,
The quaint stiff metres of olden France.

A troubadour with a whip for his lance,
In his rude calash his song betrays
Metres that speak of duel and dance.

Strange, is it not, by a happy chance
I should hear in the streets of Ste. Thérèse,
The quaint stiff metres of olden France,
Metres that speak of duel and dance ?

II.

The tall twin towers of the grim *église*
    Loom up over the wharf and street,
Over the Lombardy poplar trees.

Whichever way one goes one sees
    The *séminaire,* and is sure to meet
The tall twin towers of the grim *église,*

And but for the keen Canadian breeze
    Blowing the sharp Canadian sleet
Over the Lombardy poplar trees

To me and Pierre, who says it will freeze
    By night, I feel as if I must greet
The tall twin towers of the grim *église*

For an Old World church with Old World fees,
    The Old World *carillon* sounding sweet
Over the Lombardy poplar trees.

Vite donc, my Pierre ! For the time it flees ;
    Once more would I see from my snug low seat
The tall twin towers of the grim *église*
Over the Lombardy poplar trees.

AT ST. REMI.

I think of a land far over sea
    When I view the purple iris blooms,
The land of the golden fleur-de-lis.

When Susette in her earrings of filigree
    Dons her cap and shoulders her brooms,
I think of a land far over sea.

When I watch Nanon and old Marie,
    I seem to view in the whirring looms
The land of the golden fleur-de-lis.

When Francois-Xavier *McCartie*
    Sings as he strides across the booms,
I think of a land far over sea—

'Tis ever the same at St. Remi,
    They all suggest, both girls and grooms,
The land of the golden fleur-de-lis!

Vanish—each fir, each prim pine tree,
Vanish—the wilds with their wintry glooms—
I think instead of a land over sea,
The land of the golden fleur-de-lis.

PETITE STE. ROSALIE.

Father Couture loves a fricassee,
    Serv'd with a sip of home-made wine,
He is the Curé, so jolly and free,

And lives in Petite Ste. Rosalie.
    On Easter Sunday when one must dine,
Father Couture loves a fricassee.

No stern ascetic, no stoic is he,
    Preaching a rigid right divine.
He is the Curé, so jolly and free,

That while he maintains his dignity,
    When Lent is past and the weather is fine,
Father Couture loves a fricassee.

He kills his chicken himself—*on dit,*
    And who is there dare the deed malign?
He is the Curé, so jolly and free.

Open and courteous, fond of a fee,
    The village deity, bland and benign,
Father Couture loves a fricassee,
He's a sensible Curé, so jolly and free!

AT CAP SANTE.

I.

I ask'd to-day, "how old is the bride?"
  And they told me, quick, and true, and straight.
Jeannette has no need her age to hide,

But says "fourteen" with an air of pride.
  Now if in town at the gray church gate
I should ask to-day how old is the bride,

Would Lilian's friends the truth confide,
  Or me would they fain execrate?
Jeannette has no need her age to hide.

Her eyes met mine as her hat I tied,
  Frank eyes, that smil'd with an air sedate
When I ask'd to-day—how old is the bride?

Fourteen! Just think! Ye belles, aside!
  Bid envy swift capitulate!
Jeannette has no need her age to hide.

Heigho! those calm dark eyes! I sigh'd,
  When musing much on the holy estate,
I ask'd to-day—how old is the bride?
Jeannette has no need *her* age to hide.

II.

They'll keep it up for a week, they say,
    The wedding, I mean, of Jules and Jeannette
'Tis the proper thing at Cap Santé.

The cousins will come from Nicolet,
    From Batiscan, from Joliette,
They'll keep it up for a week, they say.

And dance and fiddle and sing away,
    Marie-Anne, Max, Léon, Lisette,
'Tis the proper thing at Cap Santé,

And they come prepar'd for the merry fray,
    They're fond of Jules, they *adore* Jeannette—
They'll keep it up *for a week,* they say.

Well! they're a hard-work'd lot though gay,
    And doubtless earn what fun they get;
'Tis the proper thing, at Cap Santé,

But we—who would put it through in a day,
    We dullards are by doubts beset.
They'll keep it up for a week, *they say,*
'Tis the proper thing at Cap Santé.

THE BEGGARS OF COTE BEAUPRE.

Here they come, whining and wailing, the Beggars of
    Côte Beaupré!
Lazy as limp Lazzaroni, an indigent herd,
Mouthing and mumbling and making a hell of the
    free highway.

Trembling, importunate, ragged, each in his vile array,
Blear-ey'd and bloodshot, both vision and intellect
    blurr'd,
Here they come, whining and wailing, the Beggars of
    Côte Beaupré.

" After " some very old master, a Teniers or Dyck in
    his day,
Perfect in patches, in palms all horny and furr'd,
Mouthing and mumbling and making a hell of the
    free highway;

Limping and lounging and breathing the breath of their
    own decay,
Each as the ghost of the other, frail shell and foul sherd,
Here they come, whining and wailing, the Beggars of
    Côte Beaupré.

Or Sidon, or Tyre, or Capernaum never were wont
    to display
More pure archetypal road paupers by no man deterr'd,
Mouthing and mumbling and making a hell of the
    free highway.

Brushing the red-fruited orchards all laden with apples
    so gay,
And harbouring many a butterfly, many a bird, .
Here they come, whining and wailing, the Beggars of
    Côte Beaupré,
Mouthing and mumbling and making a hell of the
    free highway.

STE. ANNE DE BEAUPRE.

I.

In the sacred hamlet of Bonne Ste. Anne
    One is never far from the Wayside Cross,
One is always near some talisman,

For relics, preserv'd on a famous plan
    Abound, nor suffer change or loss
In the sacred hamlet of Bonne Ste. Anne.

There, since the century first began,
    The crucifix stands, o'ergrown with moss;
One is always near some talisman,

Some skull that the poor devout may scan,
    Some bone that glows with a wonderful gloss,
In the sacred hamlet of Bonne Ste. Anne.

For a tooth, or a toe, the caravan
    Of pilgrims away its life would toss—
One is always near some talisman!

Here are the nails half buried in bran!
    Here is the corner Wayside Cross!
In the sacred hamlet of Bonne Ste. Anne
One is always near *some* talisman.

II.

Follow, follow the Pilgrims, hastening down to their
    shrine,
Dusty and worn their garments, weary their feet . . .
Hastening fast to the fane by the edge of the brine.

Talisman nought but earthy, the earthy immers'd in
    divine . . .
What does it matter? We scent the wilderness sweet,
Follow, follow the Pilgrims, hastening down to their
    shrine.

Brittany! Hearken and wonder! Your children's chil-
    dren incline,
Passing the Host as it moveth along the street,
Hastening fast to the fane by the edge of the brine.

Under the shade of a stately, a mighty Canadian pine,
Miracles daily are done and Rome is complete . . .
Follow, follow the Pilgrims, hastening down to their
    shrine!

Mother of Churches who sets for her children's children
    such wine
Giveth them also strange and miraculous meat . . .
Hastening fast to the fane by the edge of the brine,

Mother of Churches, of Nations! we also, we fall into
    line,
Follow the blind and the lame, the frail and the fleet,
Follow, follow the Pilgrims, hastening down to their
    shrine,
Hastening fast to the fane by the edge of the brine.

AT ST. BARTHELEMI.

In the parish of St. Barthélèmi
    There is always something taking place,
A procession, a fête, or a jubilee,

Some kind of religious revelry
    That pleases the fervid populace
In the parish of St. Barthélèmi.

The saints must each be remember'd. you see,
    Which perfectly suits the Gallic race . . .
A procession, a fête, or a jubilee,

Fix'd by the Church's fast decree,
    Makes them both happy and full of grace.
In the parish of St. Barthélèmi

You will easily learn to bow the knee,
    And each in its turn you will straight embrace—
A procession, a fête, or a jubilee.

In fact, there is always on the *tapis*,
    Moving at mediæval pace,
In the parish of St. Barthélèmi,
A procession, a fête, or a jubilee.

ST. JEAN B'PTISTE.

I.

'Tis the day of the blessed St. Jean B'ptiste,
　　And the streets are full of the folk awaiting
The favourite French-Canadian feast.

One knows by the bells which have never ceas'd,
　　Since early morn reverberating,
'Tis the day of the blessed St. Jean B'ptiste.

Welcome it! Joyeux, the portly priest!
　　Welcome it! Nun, at your iron grating!
The favourite French-Canadian feast.

Welcome it! Antoine, one of the least
　　Of the earth's meek little ones, meditating
On the day of the blessed St. Jean B'ptiste,

On the jostling crowd that has swift increas'd
　　Behind him, before him, celebrating
The favourite French-Canadian feast.

He is cloth'd in the skin of some savage beast.
　　Who cares if he be near suffocating?
'Tis the day of the blessed St. Jean B'ptiste,
The favourite French-Canadian Feast.

II.

Poor little Antoine! He does not mind.
It is all for the church, for a grand good cause,
The nuns are so sweet and the priests so kind.

The martyr's spirit is fast enshrin'd
In the tiny form that the ox-cart draws,
Poor little Antoine, he does not mind.

Poor little soul, for the cords that bind
Are stronger than ardor for fame or applause—
The nuns are so sweet and the priests so kind.

And after the fête a feast is design'd—
Locusts and honey are both in the clause—
Brave little Antoine! He does not mind

The heat, nor the hungry demon twin'd
Around his vitals that tears and gnaws,
The nuns are so sweet and the priests so kind.

The dust is flying. The streets are lin'd
With the panting crowd that prays for a pause.
Poor little Antoine! *He* does not mind!
The nuns are *so sweet* and the priests *so kind,*

AT STE. ROSE.

How the days are long at little Ste. Rose,
    Long in the leaf-time, long in July,
Very long when the winter sunshine glows!

In Xmas week when the shops disclose
    To the people in town grand things to buy,
How the days are long at little Ste. Rose!

"Yes!" pouts Corinne, with her little nose
    At the window pane, "it is long!" (with a sigh)
"Very long when the winter sunshine glows,

And there is but Josephe and *mon oncle* who doze,
    And nothing outside but the snow and the sky—
How the days are long at little Ste. Rose.

I can tell you—quick!" Ah, the fierce little pose
    Of the petulant puss who the Fates would defy!
What! Long when the winter sunshine glows,

In the spring time too? Now I think if she chose,
    I would willingly turn aside and try
If the days *are* long at little Ste. Rose,
Very long when the winter sunshine glows.

AT ST. HILAIRE.

Combien des enfans? Why, twenty-five!
Now, by all the Gods and every Saint,
I wonder the woman is left alive

To tell the tale! How many survive?
She answers me, calm and without constraint,
"*Combien? Mossieu?* Why, twenty-five."

Not *one* ever lost? Not one; they thrive,
Do little ones in this parish quaint.
I wonder the woman is left alive,

Who has less than twelve. The bigger the hive,
The greater the honour, no sign of complaint—
Combien des enfans? Why, twenty-five.

The men don't care and the priests contrive
At mass the duty of parents to paint,
But I wonder the women are left alive.

Here come Antoine, Josephte, Max, who drive
The rest—fifteen. At the sight you faint.
Combien des enfans? Why, twenty-five!
I wonder the woman is left alive.

AT STE. SCHOLASTIQUE.

I.

The faint warm glimpse of an olive cheek
    We catch in the light of the evening sun
At a casement in Ste. Scholastique.

By a profile perfect if hardly Greek
    We are not alone dismay'd, undone—
The faint warm glimpse of an olive cheek,

Do other travellers wistfully seek,
    And scholars some terrible risks have run
'Neath a casement in Ste. Scholastique.

The tint is so rich—the hair so sleek!
    As the curtains move, the glimpse is won,
The faint warm glimpse of an olive cheek!

Can it be, as they say, that in less than a week
    That black–hair'd nymph will pose as a nun
At a casement in Ste. Scholastique?

That Nanon will merge into Marie meek?
    If so, pass on, and devoutly shun
The faint warm glimpse of an olive cheek
At a casement in Ste. Scholastique.

II.

The World, the Flesh, and the Devil—they're
    On the country road, in the gas-lit town,
Anear and afar and everywhere.

When Nanon sets a spray in her hair,
    Or pins a rose on her homespun gown,
The World, the Flesh and the Devil are there!

And no one escapes the triune snare,
    Nor Faust, nor Fool, nor King nor Clown.
Anear and afar and everywhere

They weave and whisper and never spare
    Either labouring man or man of renown.
The World, the Flesh and the Devil—they're

Even within the wall four-square
    Of Nanon's convent. They fume and frown
Anear and afar and everywhere!

Sweet soul! Hearken well to the oath you swear
    While girl-like you grasp the coveted Crown,
For the World, the Flesh and the Devil—they're
Anear, and afar, and everywhere.

CATHARINE PLOUFFE.

This gray–hair'd spinster, Catharine Plouffe—
    Observe her, a contrast to convent chits,
At her spinning wheel, in the room in the roof!

Yet there are those who believe that the hoof
    Of a horse is nightly heard as she knits—
This gray–hair'd spinster, Catharine Plouffe—

Stockings of fabulous warp and woof,
    And that old Benedict's black pipe she permits
At her spinning wheel, in the room in the roof,

For thirty years. So the gossip. A proof
    Of her constant heart? Nay. No one twits
This gray–hair'd spinster, Catharine Plouffe;

The neighbours respect her but hold aloof,
    Admiring her back as she steadily sits
At her spinning wheel, in her room in the roof.

Will they ever marry? Just ask her. Pouf!
    She would like you to know she's not lost her wits—
This gray–hair'd spinster, Catharine Plouffe,
At her spinning wheel in the room in the roof! .

BENEDICT BROSSE.

I.

Hale, and though sixty, without a stoop,
    What does old Benedict want with a wife?
Can he not make his own pea soup?

Better than most men—never droop
    In the August noons when storms are rife?
Hale, and though sixty, without a stoop,

Supreme in the barn, the kitchen, the coop,
    Can he not use both broom and knife?
Can he not make his own pea soup?

Yet Widow Gouin in command of the troop
    Of gossips, can tell of the spinsters' strife.
Hale, and though sixty, without a stoop,

There's a dozen would jump through the golden hoop,
    For he's rich, and hardy for his time of life,
—Can he not make his own pea soup?

But Benedict's wise and the village group
    He ignores, while he smokes and plays on his fife.
Hale, and though sixty, without a stoop,
Can he not make his own pea soup?

II.

As for Catharine—now, *she's* a woman of sense,
    Though hard to win, so Benedict thinks,
Though hard to please and near with the pence.

Down to the widow Rose Archambault's fence
    Her property runs and Benedict winks—
As for Catharine—now, she's a woman of sense.

At times he has wished to drop all pretense
    And ask her—she's fond of a bunch of pinks,
Though hard to please and near with the pence,

But he never progresses—the best evidence
    That from *medias res* our Benedict Shrinks.
As for Catharine—now, she's a woman of sense,

A woman of rarest intelligence;
    She manages well, is as close as the sphinx,
Though hard to please and near with the pence.

Still, that is a virtue at St. Clements.
    Look at Rose Archambault, the improvident minx!
As for Catharine now, *she's* a woman of sense,
Though hard to please and near with the pence.

PARENTHESE AND ADIEU.

Well! 'tis over. Good-bye, Jeannette!
Good-bye, Nanon, and you, my pet,
Natalie—child of the dancing eye,
Chère Natalie, good-bye, good-bye!
Farewell—for a while, each spire-deckt town,
Each slip of a girl, so lithe and brown,
Each rushing river, each mountain mere,
Each vesper bell, so haunting clear!
Farewell, Madelon, farewell, Corinne,
And M'mselle Plouffe, so tall and thin!
Before we visit your shores again
Old Hymen you may entertain,
And now, to please us, pray let us know
If it really happens—thus—and—so.
A piece of red satin for Sunday wear,
Some stout white lace that will never tear,
An ostrich plume of a vivid green,
Some red glass earrings fit for a queen,
A pair of blue kids and a nickel chain—
These you shall have. In return we fain
Would purchase a few of your home-made chairs—
Those neat little rocker'd light wooden affairs—
Some home-made flannel, some knitted socks,
Some seeds of your double purple stocks,
And—if you will—of your hollyhocks.
We know, *mes filles,* this is much to demand,
For the latter came from that gracious land,

Your own *belle France* in the long ago,
Brought by your sires from St. Malo.
So farewell, Natalie, farewell, child—
The summer is passing, the birds fly south,
And we who were for a time beguil'd
By a laughing eye, by a mocking mouth,
We pass with the summer, we fly like the birds,
And phrases are empty—no comfort in words.
Shall you be still our sweet Natalie
When we come next year, just as free and gay,
Just as fond of the dance and the fête and the play?
We ask it, you know, since maidens like you
Are rare in the Vale of the Richelieu,
And they marry so young—there's your friend Jeannette
Is only fourteen, and you, my pet,
Are one year older already—ah! stay
At the "Sacred Heart" for a year and a day
Before you consent. "Consent! *Ma foy!*
You think, I suppose, that I like *that boy*,
Mdme. Brosse's Alphonse!!" Why, you *know* you do,
So promise, *ma mie,* when he comes to woo,
You will send him home to his own Berthier,
And keep him there for a year and a day.

L'ENVOI.

Friend, these simple rhymes forgive!
I do not ask that they should live
In your memory or your mind;
If within your heart enshrin'd
I shall deem that Fate was kind.
Simple, nay, imperfect too,
Judge them—as you're free to do.
But the while you lightly blame
Rhymes that bear a Gallic name,
Carping at the foreign metre,
Thinking English had been sweeter,
Let at least each sparkling rill,
Each quaint church upon a hill,
And a quainter people still
Charm you, friend, to near forgetting
All the poorness of the setting.
Read my *cantefable* chiefly
For its subject. Yet—and briefly—
Read it—'tis Montaigne's own line—
" Not because 'tis good, but—mine."

Thus I send these fifty-two
Simple rhymes, my friend, to you.

FROM THE PINE TO THE ROSE.

VICTORIA REGINA.

All through London's mighty maze
    Rolled the tide of Jubilee,
From her dark and sordid ways
    Came the children out to see
England's Queen of fifty years.
Beat the heart and fell the tears,
    As with martial fire and blaze,
    Pomp and pageantry and praise,
    Rolled the tide of Jubilee!

All along the mighty maze
    Rolled the Pageant of our Queen.
There was not in ancient days
    Fairer Pageant ever seen.
Withered, hangs the Tudor Rose,
All the glimmering past but shows
    Faded in the glorious blaze
    Of these late Victorian days—
    Roll—the Pageant of our Queen!

    *   *   *   *   *   *   *

In the fulness of her time,
    All her children bow and meet
In a Jubilee of rhyme,
    Cheer of army, shout of fleet!

She has seen the greatest die,
She has felt their souls pass by;
    She has heard a nation weep
    For an Iron Duke asleep,
For a Gordon in his prime—
Hark! from each colonial clime,
        Rings a cry through London street.

Rings, till chokes the London cry,
    Silence, guns, and silence, wheels!
Let her distant sons draw nigh,
    Till our loyal anthem peals
        Far from blue Canadian sky,
Pierces through the gray old pile,
Back along the Strand a mile
    Echoes over Dome and Tower
    Love for love and dower for dower,
    Hers—the right to love and power;
Her—to whom our anthem peals,
    Thunders, till her woman's heart,
Womanly, though queenly, reels.

Lo! Victoria! We bring
    Love and brave fidelity.
This believe, that with us sing
    Lovers of the *fleur-de-lis.*

Lovers of the Island Green,
Kneel with us in earnest mien,
This believe; though faults of youth
Seem to dull the edge of Truth,
Dim the Şun of Loyalty.

For should race dissension spread
Thick and deep as falls our snow,
It should ne'er of us be said
That we could let England—go.
No! Heart with heart and hand in hand
All Englishmen would make a stand
For Honour and the dear Old Land,
And ever deem her own their foe.

* * * * * * *

So through London's crowded street
Loud the younger voices rang;
Of the Polar pines and sleet,
Of the Prairie wide they sang;
From the sands of the Soudan,
From the sultry airs that fan
Egypt, India—from the Cape—
From the thronging states that shape
A second Britain in the West
Came the offering of their best.

Nay, the whole round world awoke,
High a cloud of incense broke,
Reverent greeting fond and free
To the Queen of fifty years;
Beat the hearts and fell the tears,
As with martial fire and blaze,
Pomp and pageantry and praise,
Rolled the tide of Jubilee!

* IN THE QUEEN'S PARK, MAY 24th, 1887.

Come! What are ye waitin' there for?
    Don't ye 'ear what the people say?
Don't ye want to join the procession?
    Don't ye know it's the Queen's Birthday?
If *I* was the one as faltered,
    And grumbled and looked kind o' black,
It might be forgiven me, surely,
    With ninety years at my back.
· But there! I'm as willin' as ever,
    Although I can't 'ear 'em play,
To join with the band in singin'
    "God Save 'Er" on 'er Birthday!

She's sixty-eight and I'm ninety;
    We're both gettin' on, I know.
She's the Dook o' Kent's little daughter,
    I mind 'er openin' show.
'Twas in the black old Abbey—
    How the London crowd did pour
'Long the Strand from dock and City
    And cheered 'er at the door!
And I was there, and your father,
    And we both elbowed our way
To the side o' the Royal Carriage
    On the Coronation Day!

* On the occasion of the trooping of the colours by Lord Lansdowne.

She give us a smile, I remember,
　　And we come away satisfied.
I see 'er next at 'er weddin,
　　With Prince Albert at 'er side.
I did'nt sulk and grumble
　　As some o' you young uns do,
I'd been used to crowds 'afore—why, boy!
　　I was at Waterloo;
And in crowds, mind, do as I do,
　　Just push and fight your way,
Or ye'll find—'ere, boy! your arm, lad!
　　Pretty work on a Queen's Birthday!

They had almost ridden me down like,
　　'Tis a pity old folks can't 'ear,
But my sight is as good as ever,
　　And there goes a Grenadier!
A splendid fellow he is, too—
　　A chip off the fine old block,
And 'ere is the Governor-General,
　　Sharp to his 'leven o'clock!
Ay, ay, but it takes me back, lad,
　　And England seems far away,
And I wish I could cheer as I'd like to
　　For 'er Sixty-Eighth Birthday.

.

But you—why, I'm 'alf ashamed o' ye!
   Ye don't give as lusty a cheer
As me with my bent old shoulders,
   As me with my ninety year!
Ye've got hold o' new ideas;
   " Beant English "—well, that may be;
Ye " wasn't born in England,"—
   But your father was—and me,
And ye live in the Queen's Dominions,
   And ye owe her every way,
And it's nothin' more than your duty
   To cheer on the Queen's Birthday.

For what if your mother was Irish,
   And what if ye don't just like
The ways o' some around ye,
   And feel sort o' set on strike!
Take me—I come out in—'40
   To this 'ere Canadian land,
And there's many things as I know
   I don't yet 'alf understand,—
Why the Quality's twice as 'aughty,
   Why the Parks must be sold away,
And why ye must drink in water
   'Er 'ealth on the Queen's Birthday.

But though I'm a loyal Briton
    I love the new land too.
What's this O'Brien? Who's he
    To meddle with me and you?
'Tis a fair young land in truth, lad,
    Look around, and ye'll see how fair,
With the glory o' spring-time grasses,
    With the chestnut smell in the air.
Why, a prettier spot than this, lad,
    And people in finer array
Could 'ardly be found in Old England,
    A-keepin the Queen's Birthday!

And we look to all you youngsters
    To keep your land fair and young,
To take no man for a leader
    As hasn't an honest tongue.
There! Watch the eddykongs gallop,
    And 'ark to a British cheer!
Get me a better place, lad —
    I wish your "O'Brien" was 'ere!
And I wish that the Queen 'erself was
    Able to see the display,
And the loyal crowds as is keepin'
    'Er Sixty-Eighth Birthday!

ENGLAND.

The Lark at dawn, the Nightingale at eve
Conspire to make it beautiful. I had dreamed
Of some such Beauty—lo! it rose around me
More exquisite than any dream, more fair,
Than even the favourite dreams of cherished children,
And what those are—how strange, how sweet, how rare,
We all remember—when a touch, a sound,
        Startles us, and we look
Backwards—ten, twenty, thirty, forty years.
        Yet fairer even than those
        Cloud-visions capped with rose,
My England—with her abbeys framed in green;
Gray Tintern set not too far from the sea
By subtle monks, safe in its rim of hills,
And gayer Furness, clad in mellow reds
That glimmer warm through many an ivy-mat,
And tall cathedrals tipped with shimmering spires,
        That hang over hut and hall,
        And satin poppies, scarlet, wild,
Clasped in the hands of the labourer's child,
And tangled cottage gardens gaily drest
In all their rustic Sunday summer best.
        O blame them not who evermore
        Upon a cold colonial shore
Feel their hearts burn within them at the thought

Of all that Beauty! Let it be said of such—
Not that they loved their Canada the less
But only—England—the more. Let it be said
Of them, that nature did so feed their souls
With all that was grand, illimitable, potent, fresh,
That poesy failed them. Nature was all in all;
Too self-sufficing, strong, relentless, masterful,
To aid the human spirit. Then there stole
From English valleys, leafy lanes, high hills,
From sloping uplands, farms and lichened towers,
From roofless ruins gracious in decay—
Something—a sentiment, aspiration, wish—
That soothed, inspired at once, that gave for wild
Dissatisfaction, peace. Dear England! I—
I have not—yet I fain had been—thy child!

ON DURDHAM DOWN.

I.

O who will come and view with me
The glory of the chestnut tree?

And who with me will fondly laud,
Forgetting carven ones abroad,

In London, Moscow, or in Rome,
This green and more harmonious dome?

If such a friend exist for me,
Let him make haste, come soon, that we

Together rosy rain may share,
That falls upon my cheek, my hair,

Then flutters delicately down,
Bestrews with pink the roadside brown.

II.

Choice of the chestnuts, pink or white,
Is mine and his for our delight.

III.

Then let him come with me and see
The blossoming laburnum tree.

The purest yellow in the world
Hangs from its tender green unfurled.

No poet that I know has sung
This perfect yellow downward flung—

Indeed, no poet that I know,
From out his heart's glad overflow,

Has sung, as I should like to sing,
The splendours of an English spring.

Is it revealed to me this day
To be the priestess of the May,

The next, the fairest that we see,
The best beloved of any tree,

The hawthorn—pink, and white, and red,
That sometimes stretches overhead,

And sometimes grows so low, so low,
That I can touch it as I go?

To be the poet of the May,
Were cause enough to wear the bay,

And wear it humbly, since I see
For the first time the hawthorn tree.

IV.

When first it wears its snow-white crown,
A lovely sight is Durdham Down!

The bloom is piled like drifting snow!
I think, if some slight wind should blow,

It would arise and fly away,
It seems too light, too soft, to stay!

And well it is the sun is paled
So often in this land mist-veiled.

Should once his natural fire be felt,
The bloom would slowly, surely melt !

But soon it proves itself a flower
That crowns the Down with snowy dower,

For here and there the red May shows
As rich a crimson as the rose,

And last, there wakes for new delight,
Another sense than that of sight,

For sweeter e'en than new-mown hay
Is blown the fragrance of the May,

And I am happy—since I see
For the first time the hawthorn tree !

TINTERN ABBEY.

To wear its image—seal'd—fix'd mentally,
Pinn'd to my heart's eyes – old, smooth-worn, gray stone,
Green-lichen'd, ivy-curtain'd, blossom-blown
In stray sweet crevices—this is fealty !
O, I could never look enough, but see
Some new divinity each second, grown
By the potent centuries—guardians. There, alone,
Girdled by hills it rested, and to me
The great rose window form'd a glorious fane,
Mightier than other I had ever seen,
And when I lifted awed eyes, finite brain
To the open blue, where once a roof had been,
I knew from innumerable, awful winnowings- -
There was more room for our great God's wide wings.

TO MAURICE THOMPSON.

I.

I wage a war with you who sang
Your song of England. That it rang

Through England, doubt not, for the song
So tender was, so sadly strong,

I surely think that long ere this,
The looked-for, long expected bliss

Is yours, and that they must have come
To tell you England called you home.

II.

For you on England have a claim,
'Tis meet that she should know your name,

The last of all her archer-race—
For you must be a trysting-place.

Surely for you a welcome waits,
Surely for you are opened gates,

And Christmas cheer, and hearth-side kiss,
And what you value more than this,

The merry horns that roam the wood,
And rouse the merry hunting mood.

O even as I write, perchance,
Maid Marian leads you forth to dance;

A modern Marian, well I know,
But sweet as she who bent the bow

In Sherwood once with Robin Hood.
Perchance already you have stood

Knee-deep in English grass and fern,
And felt your arrow in its turn

Leap like a prisoner to the air,
Who had forgotten earth was fair.

Was this your dream? And have they come
To tell you England calls you home?

III.

And this is why I wage my war,
And this is why I sing afar

From land of pines and snowy land,
—All, all is snow on every hand,

And gray and white are all I see,
Or white or gray alike to me—

To one who in a warmer clime
Blows the bright bubble of his rhyme,

And plies his task with half a heart,
Standing from other men apart

That he may sooner catch the words,
More welcome far than mating birds

In this drear north—the words that burn
With exile past and sweet return

Of English joys and games and glades,
And merry men and modest maids—

Because his wish was also mine,
And is and always will be mine,

The wish, the hope—to end my days
In England, and with English ways

Once more to feel a calm content,
Once more to thrill with sentiment,

Born of her myths and mystery,
Born of her wondrous history,

And of her beauty—ah! I swear
I know not anything more fair

In this new land of clearer skies,
Than English mists that shyly rise

From off shy streams or ivied walls.
Or cling about fair ruined halls,

Too fondly true to keep away,
Too truly fond too long to stay,

And O—for glimpse of English green,
I well could give my soul, I ween.

I never pulled a primrose, I,
But could I know that there may lie

E'en now some small and hidden seed
Below, within, some English mead,

Waiting for sun and rain to make
A flower of it for my poor sake,

I then could wait till winds should tell
For me there swayed or swung a bell,

Or reared a banner, peered a star,
Or curved a cup in woods afar.

A grave in England! Surely there
In churchyard ancient, quiet, fair,

My rest may some sweet day be found,
And I shall sleep in tranquil ground,

While English violets bloom anear,
—But who am I?   And who may hear

My prayer, and where the friends to come
And tell me England calls me home?

IV.

I am no merry archer bold—
In sooth, I know not how to hold

A bow and arrow!   This your claim,
O friend in Florida, to fame,

I ne'er will question.   Singer too
Of noble songs!   I have, 'tis true,

A little written, some things done,
But dare not hope that any one

Of my poor ventures e'er shall gain
The listening ear of England, fain

To know the deeds her children do
And merge her old life in our new.

V.

And shall I quarrel with you, then,
Because I envy you the pen,

The bow and arrow? Nay, not so,
For that would ill accord with flow

Of yearning tears and brow tight clasped,
And words in swift confusion gasped,

Because I read your verses, friend.
Nay, why a quarrel? I but send

These lines to you that you may know
Your lines to one soul straight did go,

And dare to hope that when the boon
You long for comes, (and that full soon

I know must be, and they will come
To tell you England calls you home)

You will remember when you see
A pale new primrose deck the lea,

How one who lives in northern lands,
Would pluck the same with trembling hands,

And meanwhile wonder how she dare,
If she were there—if she were there!

VI.

And now I charge you, when the call
Rings in your ears and down you fall

Only to rise with hastening feet
And press towards the ocean sweet,

No more a barrier but a bridge,
And later, when you see the ridge

Of English land low-lying white,
Or Welsh hills topped with quivering light—

See that you faint not, let your heart
Full thankful be that yet a part

In England's history you can play,
That England needs her son to-day.

VII.

My words are vain. I know ere this
The looked-for, long expected bliss

Is yours and that they must have come
To tell you England calls you home.

A MONODY.

.

A MONODY.

TO THE MEMORY OF ISABELLA VALANCY CRAWFORD.

I weep for our dead Sappho—Sappho, who is dead,
    Was ours, and great, although her friends were few;
Let the great Greek go by, or lift in love her laurelled
        head,
    One of her peers hath entered; let her view
The youngest poet-soul that darkly gropes
    For light and truth; let the great Greek outstretch
    Warm hands of welcome, Deity-bidden, fetch
The faint soul home with Love's strong coilèd ropes.

I weep for our dead Sappho—Sappho, who was ours,
    The great Greek knew her, shame—that we did not;
Did not her songs pierce blue, light dark and break through
        close-branched bowers?
    Yet was an early grave her earthward lot.
Whom the gods love die young. Great Sappho, raise
    Thy yearning arms and draw her from the flood;
    Cheer thou her spirit, warm her freezing blood,
Lave her faint brow, and crown it with clinging bays.

I make my moan the while. I do not weep
    Because that Death her body hath not spared;
Weep I for thoughts of bliss, of converse sweet with
        meaning deep,
    That, had I known her, surely we had shared.
I weep for thinking much of the forest walks,
    When willows shimmer with leaf of thinnest gold,
    And crumpled green is ready to unfold,
And white show all the slender reedy stalks

Within the muddy marshes; here and there,
    A stray wind-flower that stars the sunny glade,
A triple-leafed trillium tall, that soon in May-time light
        shall wear
    Its white flower—lovely lamp for lanes of shade.
I weep for thinking much of the purple blooms
    We might have seen together on the hills,
    The while the melting snow made rough the rills,
And from the frozen flats uprose the glooms.

I weep, and wonder much who was her friend;
    Or had she none, and so crept unconsoled
Lonely along life's sunless shore and sadly, bravely penned
    The lines that read so warm, that ring so bold.
As water precious sediment, shining ore,
    So the clear liquid of her verse embalms,
    Like amber, flies—the fire, the flush, the palms
Of passionate tropics, pulsing, sun-bathed shore.

I make my moan the while. I weep to think
    Such walks were not for us, nor yet that hour
Far dearer still to friends when snow hath curtained every
        chink,
    And hearth-sides blaze with welcome, though there
        lower
The God of Storm upon the threshold neat.
    To have sat so—close and tender; (women can—
    Are all to themselves, and happy, need no man,)
Alas! that we never lit on such retreat!

Such solace there was none. Great Sappho—raise
    Her drooping head and tell her one hath come,
Late though it seem, with yearning words of comfort
        and of praise!
    She does not hearken. Yet she is but dumb.
Wait but a little—she will sing again.
    I wait. I watch the trees fire, one by one,
    I count the oxen, indolent in the sun,
I see the sparkle of many a distant vane.

I smooth the chestnuts shining in the grass,
    I look up when a bird is felt to whir—
These are my truest joys. O wherefore comes it thus to pass
    That these are no more anything to her?
This day is like her—sumptuous, vivid, warm,
    All golden mellow, gemmed with spots of fire.
    Demeter, smiling, 'ere she slay desire
With warring winds and icy breath of storm

Hath cast upon the earth a veil of gold,
    Defying Danaë. *I, too, work my spells.*
Zeus is not only lord. Behold the vales, the slopes behold,
    The woods of bronze, the topaz-sprinkled dells !
The myths still live. I am not shrunken yet,
    Disabled, no, nor impotent, failing, weak ;
    'Tis I who crumple claw, form flower, ope beak,
Knit cobweb, paint the maples, frost-snares set.

Thus the sly Goddess. Every year she makes
    The simple Earth most beautiful for a time.
But, every year, dread mother, her revenge unguessed
        she slakes,
    When green and gold are gone, with sleet and rime.
Thus doth she make her moan. Persephone
    Dieth once a year to life and light and air,
    Howbeit she lives afar, most strangely fair,
With eyes that in the dark have learnt to see.

Here, where the leaves are trodden inches deep,
    What waste of colour, symmetry, beauty, life !
There, where her soul's rich song is hushed in waiting,
        wavering sleep,
    We dare not figure waste. Across the strife
That strangles Hope ever high at the court of God,
    That voice at last shall be clearly, daily heard,
    That heart with holiest striving shall be stirred,
That soul be free to soar, as lark from sod.

.

Yet are we mocked by cold conjecture's wraith!
To sigh and grasp at what is gone for aye—
I too, Earth-mother, lose my calm, I lose my saving faith,
I too, disdain the world's vile disarray
And would avenge its blindness, point its shame.
Kill off for me, Demeter, thus I cry,
These impotent — that the great, good gods defy,
These flies of men that dally with her name!

For her's was no slight soul. Kind Sappho knows—
For she hath read those Greek-inspirèd lines,
Stanzas in which as of old the Spartan spirit steadily
glows—
Deep—as Ægean blue through branching vines,
Strong—as the naked limbs of Spartan youth,
Hot—as the suns on Ætolia's rocky plains.
Clasp me the *Helot*—reach me the rich quatrains,
That throb with triumph, touched with the wand of truth!

I make my moan the while. Dear Sappho—list!
Ask her this, further. Was she loath to go,
Or was she ready, willing, soul-enchanted since she wist
Not fully of her gift, nor of life below?
Nay—so the calm Greek whispers—*'tis no time*
To question her. For a soul so lately riven
By Death's slow pains, though fully, know, forgiven,
May answer not. Ponder then in your heart your rhyme.

I wait. I watch the Autumn. Swift it passes,
 Till sallow fungi stud the dripping trees;
Brittle and brown and dry grow even the smoothest,
  greenest grasses,
 And garden-plots lie naked to the breeze,
And rifled rigging climbeth the damp dull house,
 And men and women crouching before their fire,
 Hearken the wind as it climbeth ever higher,
Hearken the cricket, watch for the keen-eyed mouse.

Four walls hath bound them—bound me too, the same,
 Not like that spirit —bursting place and age,
The mummy-like cloths of genius—that pure fire, that
  golden flame,
 Her lambent thought, that fed each splendid page
With picturesque portraits, Greek, Italian, Spanish.
 The pomp of Rome, the clash of Capitol hate,
 La Bouquetière, sweet victim of foul fate—
How beside these do colder visions vanish!

Four walls could not her feverish spirit fetter,
 Yet precious airs strove with her, sweet, unsought;
Often I think, that had I called her friend or known
  her better,
 I might have steered the rich barque of her thought
To shores of our own, looming softly, freshly fair.
 I might have shown her—tawny eastern torrents,
 The lonely Gatineau, the vast St. Lawrence.
I might have said—*In all this thou shalt share;*

Take it, and make it—thou who only can'st,
Sweet alchemist—rare singer—what thou wilt ;
Distilled in thine alembic, earth-dissevered, as thou
    plann'st,
Our life's ideal shalt on thee be built.
Had I but known her well—thus had I spoken.
    But now she sleeps where Sappho guards and guides,
    Deaf to the rolling in of Death's slow tides,
And Charon's ship on the black wave's crest unbroken.

There where the canyon, cut in the living rock,
    Its snow-streaked side up from the prairie lifts,
Shall not her name live long,--I think so, till Time has
        ceased to mock,
    Hath she not conquered Death by gracious gifts ?
Did she not sing the song of the pioneer,
    An epic of axe and tree, of glebe and pine,
    Hath she not—Great High Priestess of Love benign,
Rose-crowned, brow-bound, from Love dissevered Fear?

I shall not cease to moan. Some day I shall catch
    The music of the voice I wait to hear,
And hearing, rapt, declare that its magic melody doth
        not match
    With aught ever heard in this songless hemisphere.
O, could I hope that the mantle of her song
    Might fall on me through very love of her—
    Strong Sappho! Grant it! *I may not confer*
High gifts: her gifts alone to her God belong.

VIE DE BOHEME.

.

VIE DE BOHEME! OR THE NOCTURNE IN G.

(In the Latin Quarter.)

Vie de Bohême!   Curious, are you?
    Really, earnestly want to know all
About it?   Well, you needn't go far, you
    Have only to step across the hall.

This mountain of trunks outside the door!
    Perhaps you might care to investigate these,
But I'll not risk becoming a bore—
    Here, the door is open! *Entrez.*   (Sneeze!)

Snuff and scissors, and salt and Strauss—
    The last weak opera—have you seen it?—
All on a chair, and a little dead mouse
    Underneath in a trap, where the hangings screen it.

The chair itself, though, you don't see daily.
    Look at the carvings there in the middle
Of the back—all the others are occupied gaily,
    While the lounge has a tray, a dog and a fiddle.

There's nothing to sit upon—but the bed.
    "But Madame will object!"   Not she.   Asleep
At twelve of the clock!   What a heavy head!
    I'd wake her—but you are an artist,—Peep

For a minute longer at curve of wrist,
    And hair out-stretched upon the pillow!
Is there anything there that will assist
    Your latest dream of women and willow?

How sad she looks! Very sad for her,
    That never sorrows a moment awake;
Now, could you fasten that mouth's demur
    On your canvas, *mon cher*, you were made! Crimson
        lake?

And you *mouchoir* went into it? All my fault!
    I should not have entered Bohemia so,
With a sensitive Sybarite not worth his salt—
    Well, I'll take that back, and you too, if you'll go.

But not just at present. Why, pocket the stain!
    'Twill come out quite easily by-and-by;
And whether it come out, or if it remain,
    In Bohemia does not in the least signify.

Look out for your head, for the ceiling's low,
    And out of three globes on the chandelier,
Only one is left, and it's cracked, will go
    To pieces almost if one looks at it near.

.

The pinned-up blind and the breakfast tray
  Are not things wherewithal to boast,
But the Dresden and Derby in shining array,
  Will surely obliterate hardening toast,

And long-poured-out coffee. At last! She stirs!
  Madame is awake. Good-day! *" Bonjour!*
" Mon Dieu, it is late, and the friend infers
  That so late every day, I must sleep *toujours!*

" I am an object? Quick, say!" Ah, Madame!
  One of grace and delight you always must be,
And most of all now; 'tis not often *les femmes*
  Look so well upon waking. Is it, Lee.

Lee is my friend and a fast rising painter;
  Does things which outrival your matchless Corot;
Murky gray skies, with a curious fainter
  Lighter green gleam on the landscape below.

Though, is it Corot that I mean? Lee is shocked.
  Suffice it, we saw you last night in the play,
In a pink and white poem so charmingly frocked,
  O happy, thrice happy *Théâtre Français!*

He begs for a sitting, and let me suggest
    That you stay as you are with those fair frills of lace
Brimming over the coverlet—why, you *are* dressed
    With all that soft whiteness beneath your face,

And the bright bloom of Eos on either cheek,
    And a most divine violet-black in your eyes,
As liquid as childhood's—there's no need to seek
    The embrightening drugs' and the rouge-pots' lies.

But later, Madame, you'll be pale, no doubt.
    No? Not when the afternoon shadows fall,
In the *triste* interim when old loves are about,
    And old voices and footsteps are heard over all

The playing of Monsieur Diabolus? Ah!
    He is here as I speak, and now, friend Lee,
Whom I think, Chevalier, you yesterday saw
    In my room downstairs, recollect? No. 3?

We'll leave you to settle your palette and plushes,
    To frown and reflect, then to rumple your hair,
And presently actively bristle with brushes.
    So; practise, Chevalier, while I will prepare

Quelque chose pour Madame.   Not a word, my own way.
   The coffee is cold, but—I have it! *Margaux!*
In one pocket you see; in the other a stray
   Find of fresh plums and a tiny *gâteau*

Picked up at Victors.   A glorious cook!
   No Frenchman, believe me, though here in the heart
Of your Paris he works since the day he forsook
   The fluctuate fortune of Poland for Art.

You laugh, *mes amis.*   Well, it's this.   He's a Pole,
   Therefore illustrious; Poles always are;
He puts into pink butter roses his soul,
   And it is not a common one.   Follows some star

Or Muse in his cooking; is the better for blood,
   As brains always are when together you find them;
The Regent had loved him; put poison for cud
   Had Carême in his *bouquets garnis* as he twin'd
      them;

Now Chopin and he were great friends in their way,
   And Victor has told me, his ices and cakes
Of the best inspiration, *salmis, entremêts,*
   Of the rarest, he owed to the delicate shakes

And the marvellous touch of *ce pauvre Frédèric*.
   So eat up your cake, Madame, every crumb!
Value its shape and its colouring, seek
   (It is not unworthy your finger and thumb)

For its meaning, its essence—no, not the vanilla!
   Go on with your sketching, and Lee, look here!
Madame does not exile the darling Manilla,
   You may puff away with your conscience clear,

If you want to and can with this in your ears,
   The sad soul of Chopin on violin strings!
Ah! Paint me the picture the most full of tears,
   Tear your own heart out and pluck off your wings,

Let the down that was snowy and dowered as your own
   Feed your ne'er dying worm as it rears and recedes,
Let the blood that once warmed you through breast to
      cold bone
   Flow out and delight but not drown as it feeds—

Not the grave-worm, Madame— Ah! would God that it were!
   (My worm, and your's, Lee, are both of a gender),
A live thing so harmlessly, holily fair!
   No. We were enthralled with a mirage of splendour.

.

And it dies not; it dies not; it will push its way,
   And here we are, slaves to its growth and its power ;
To the worship of Art were we both called one day,
   For the worship of Art have we lived till this hour.

Feed your worm then, I say, with superlative pain,
   Paint me the picture the most full of tears—
You will never attain to that wonderful strain
   The musician alone through the hurrying years

Can give us—the wistful, the cry of all souls
   Inarticulate, helpless, abandoned and blind,
To the *Dieu inconnu,* the Unknown that controls
   All the joy and the pain of our poor human kind.

But Madame there grows restless, declares I am *triste ;*
   I am old, *chers amis,* but not cynical, no!
You have finished, I see, my ingenious feast,
   If I had now but purchased another *gâteau!*

Lee—rehearsal draws near. Say good-bye to it all,
   Come and look here, Chevalier, there's nothing to
      dread,
Ah! No colour, my friend! Take this red parasol,
   Stand it open at back of Madame's little head!

Then give her the "ruby" in one slender hand,
    Let her bury the other beneath her hair—
You've a picture the *Salon* will quite understand,
    And accept with *éclat*, for your subject is rare,

You have gone to real life, the critics will say,
    Heart, and not Art, is the luckiest creed.
Apropos, you may think of the lines that, one day,
    To you in some *café* I once tried to read.

They ran—*Now, mark me, Lee, you'll never paint
Until you learn more daring. Dare to fling
Those golden-threaded pretty stuffs away!
Strip down the flecked Madras and tear the eyes
From yonder ceiling peacock-feathered! Sell
Your china cheap and curtains, amber plush
And ruby, making sunset in the room!
I did not come to see a splash of west,
Except, I own, upon your canvas here.
Bury your bronzes—curse the bric-à-brac!
You've learned to draw it? Good! Now go your way
Into the world, the street, the omnibus,
Shall Lee—no name to conjure with as yet—
Refuse to follow where Detaille has led?*

But Madame, I digress, and the time, how it goes!
    Adieu for the present.   One wish—might I claim
This smallest, most withered, and least little rose,
    With the *beauté altière* and the difficult name?

Twelve bouquets—observe, Lee—all thrown in one night,
    Who were guilty of some would be easy to see;
Here's a note, there's a case—oh! we must take our flight,
And thanks, Chevalier, for the Nocturne in G.

" J'AI TROP BU LA VIE."

(GEORGE SAND.)

Ah! what a wonderful draught!
   Now, was it ruby red,
      With heart of flame in the glass,
   A passionate crimson shed
   By the loves on which she fed?

Or with a golden hue
   Caught from the grapes that grow
      High in the sunshine of Fame—
   Thus with an amber glow
   Did her life's elixir flow?

Or was it colourless, clear,
   White to her mortal eye,
      Pure from a mountain stream,
   Fresh from a fountain high,
   Losing itself in the sky?

Or was it none of these,
   Ripe and rare to the taste,
      Rose or gold to the eye,
   Brought in a beaker chased,
   Bearing a rim flower-graced?

But was it muddy and black?
   Bending over the brink
     Of a foul and stagnant pool,
  Loathing the draught, did she drink?
  Draining the cup, did she shrink?

What were its dregs to her?
   Ah! what a wonderful draught!
     Perhaps, as the dregs she drained,
  Perhaps, as the cup she quaffed,
  Her tempting angel laughed.

TO MIRANDA.

The paper moon of pink
Has continents of ink,
An undiscovered literary sphere.
Above your head it swings,
Above the golden rings
That drop behind and wave below and softly veil your ear.

The moon, like some large pearl,
Looms calm amid the whirl
Of hearts and stars and planets, pulses all;
The globe on which we fly,
The mimic one on high—
They both are real, and each is but a frail and wind-
chased ball.

The banners northward flung,
The silver ribbons hung
Across an amber arch that fades to green;
The flash of flying stars,
The fiery eye of Mars,
The blue of Sirius ere he drops behind that dusky screen;

The colour everywhere,
The perfume in the air,
The mystery and magic of the place;
The sweet disquietude,
With revery embued,
This is no cold colonial night—you boast some other race;

Some other clime you knew,
Some foreign land knew you
When first you shook your curls upon the wind;
In Grecian meadows sweet,
You set your girlish feet,
Or laughed in lakes Italian as the parted grass you thinned.

No daughter of the snow,
No northern bud could blow
Into a gold-crowned blossom, lace-enswathed;
The soft and sunny South
Has surely framed that mouth,
The fervid East that glowing skin, those languid limbs,
has bathed.

Although your hair be gold,
It holds no hint of cold,
But rather guards a bright and secret flame ;
I see from my low place
A curl lie on the lace—
It harbours light and warmth that put yon brazen bowl
to shame !

My place is low but near,
If I but choose I hear
The tinkle of the cross that strikes your brooch ,
The little cross—my gift—
Chimes on as if to lift
My soul to worship, while it guards and consecrates
approach.

We keep, with voices mute,
A silence absolute.
If I but choose, all's read within your eyes ;
If *you* but choose, I may
Upon your lap just lay
A hand too calm, too confident, to tremble at its prize.

So—should we float to-night
In some enchanted flight
Towards those stars that mock our mimic moon,
We need not aught exchange,
Nor find the new world strange,
Since float with us through ether to some clear and
joyous rune—

The pansy's purple dark,
The red geranium's spark,
The rosy oleander, smooth and tall ;
The world of mignonette,
The morning-glories met
By vine and sweet clematis climbing up the latticed wall ;

The white and orange fire
Of lanterns that conspire
Against the shadows stealing overhead ;
The arching horns of moose,
The awnings flapping loose,
The tawny rugs that meet your feet, and make my supple
bed ;

The swing in which you sway,
The net of gold and gray,
The hammock filled with cushions to the brim,
The wine within your hand,
Of rare and subtle brand,
The glow within your eyes, the low and long repose
of limb;—

If good enough for this
Sad world of cankered bliss,
Perverted aims, rash hopes, and weak despairs,
These essences so fine,
These flowers and scents divine,
That seek the best nor flourish save in pure and perfect airs,

If strong enough for all
The gales that rock this ball,
The northern tumults both of wind and hail,
This canopy so free,
This latticed balcony,
That near the river rears its orange-lighted nest so frail;

There is no world afar,
On planet or in star,
No mystic country Merlin ever sought,
Too fair for such a face,
For such a hidden place
Of sweetest refuge, flower and briar, pain and pleasure
fraught ;

There is no fairy realm,
Where magic at the helm
Holds back the ever reeling wheel of sense;
No charmèd gallery,
On mountain or by sea,
Where merge the nightly trances in the day-dream's joys
intense;

No turret-chamber hewn
In castle rock, and strewn
With sweetness pluckt at dawn to scent the day;
No palace shining fair,
With gleam of carven stair,
And splash of falling fountain in the courtyard cool and
gray,

Beneath what cloudless sky,
Too fair, too sweet, too high,
To shelter you, past mistress of delight!
I deem not half so fair
That royal room and rare,
Where Isolt sprang with sobs upon the breast of her lost
knight!

That room so narrow neat,
Where Hero, fair and sweet,
Caught young Leander on her outstretched arm,
And drew him to the light.
From out th' encircling night,
And clasped him close and kissed him fast till he grew
strong and warm ;

And growing warm, grew bold,
And took with passionate hold
Her paling face between his trembling hands,
And made her own that hour
The man's consummate power
To drown her voice, and break her will, and bind her
in love's bands—

O sweeter far than it,
This place wherein we sit,
And sweeter far than lips on other lips,
To close our eyes and know,
Whatever dreams may go,
The cherished one may stay, nor suffer wrong, nor fear
eclipse!

BOHEMIA.

Where's Bohemia ?—Anywhere
That Life is full and rich and rare.
Yours—a verandah,
Mine—an attic ;
Her's—a *salon*
Epigrammatic ;
Artists—of course ;
A writer or two ;
Beer and tobacco,
I fear—both due.
But music *is* music,
And art *is* art,
The Muses are happy,
Sans Mammon and Mart.
There's Cordeux, the tenor,
You've heard him—in halls,
When the impotent pianist
Accompanies him. "Calls,
Encores and *bravas*,"—
Oh ! yes, I've no doubt !
But hear him to-night
Chez Essarre and without
That tag, the accompanist,
Then you shall see
For the first time, my Cordeux,
As a god—*mon ami !*

For he strikes but a chord
    And the women are still,
Julie, Duchesse, La Riva, .
    Old Gautier and " Lil."
We don't Talk in Bohemia,
    Mark that—when you go,
But, eyes, ears—are riveted,
    Heads are bent low.
I've seen tears on occasions
    When Gounod is sung,
And Godard or Schumann.
    Last night " Renée " hung
To the Princess B's arm
    As the *Vorspiel* was played.
Her story's a tragic one.
    Brilliant—arrayed
In her third-act lace costume,
    Yet suffering—apart—
Two children in Russia,
    A spouse—without heart,
You know him—Count Dinitry.
    Such women as she
Should'nt marry. Sh! well,
    This—between you and me.

But it's high time we dined, Carl.
　　I've two francs to spare.
Come! empty your pockets—
　　Three? Lucky, *mon cher*.
Then, *après*, we'll fly
　　To Essarre's charming flat—
You shall hear some *real* music,
　　I promise you that.
And as for the goodness
　　Or badness of such
As we'll meet there—why—Carl,
　　It will not matter—much.
Take the average always
　　Of women—men too—
If the faulty are legion,
　　The good—alas—few,
'Tis out of Bohemia
　　The same—take my word!
In the village, the valley,
　　The big London herd!
Bohemia's no worse—
　　And no better— *I* think,
Than the rest of the world.
　　There's Essarre now—in pink,

On her way home to dinner,
    Old Claude by her side.
For ten years he is dumb,
    Before that the chief pride
Of the Comédie Française.
    The generous soul!
That must share with some other
    Her hard-earned rent-roll.
Yet her temper's not sweet
    If the "supers" say true—
Bah! Who is perfection?
    Not I—and not—you.
Bohemia's a medley;
    Mad virtues, sane whims;
For Gretchen plays billiards,
    While Mephisto sings hymns.
Faust patiently rocking
    A querulous child,
Is henpecked by Martha
    No matron too mild;
Rich Mdme. La Riva,
    A ballet-girl once,
Drives· daily where Costo
    Her coachman confronts.

Old Costo's her father—
    She meets him at mass,
And keeps him in clothing,
    Is his " kind, clever lass!"
To share in her greatness
    He never aspires;
Gets drunk on her earnings,
    Adores and admires.
We rise in Bohemia
    From all sorts of places,
From alien, mongrel,
    And quite tabooed races.
And where is Bohemia ?—Anywhere
    That Life is subtle—sad—*Deux Frères*
    Provençales – Pierre et George—entrez !
    I had a good meal there yesterday.

PARK ST. MAYFAIR.

(A STAR SPEAKS.)

O not to love the place where one was born,
Not even to care to see it—not to love
All early moods and friends and forms and faces,
All childish things, all books, all plays, all places
That one has known in far sequestered years—
It is a *bitter* thing! I read to-night
For the first time, the hectic ecstacies
Of Gray, the latter David, the Scotch Chatterton.
The book was sent me—'tis not known—poor boy!
Poor boy—I wept, and still in weeping felt
I envied him, he loved his cottage so,
His natal valley, Luggie's tawny -banks.
He loved them so, I say, he loved them so.
There! I am mad to-night! Women like me,
Self-wrought, self-taught, fighting the world aside,
And oh! to women the wide world *is* wide,
Ambitious, scornful, *filiae populi,*
Rare daughters of the people, rare, why not?
I brought you Art, from where all Art was nought—
Women like me in whom the wine of life
Runs madly, dowered with red of blood and lip,
With Irish blue of eye and black of hair,
Talking of cottages—Ah! Justine, I'll wear
The Felix dress to-night. Which one? The last,
That delicate dream of gray dissolved in green;

The gray alone would slay me, but the tint
Of olive in the green and then that knot
Of deep red roses—yes, 'tis well—and he,
He, Felix, is no fool. I was the first
To make him famous—mind, the night I played
My " Adrienne" first. 'Twas you?   No, 'twas Annette,
And for a week I knew not what to wear,
And for a week I cared not if I wore
Nothing—till three days past I breathless sent
To Felix. "Madame will require at once—
A *débutante*—four dresses—Lecouvreur—
Original if possible—Drury Lane—
Complexion fair, hair dark, *her own*, in height
A little above the medium, eyes dark blue."
A pretty telegram, they told Annette,
But she, a clever Frenchwoman, yes, far
Cleverer than you Justine, just turned it off.
You've seen those dresses?   One I still can wear,
The one *en Pompadour*, heart-shaped at waist,
An innocent pattern, rosebuds, wings, silk-laced,—
I wore it yesterday, you know, to Kew.
The artists were in raptures at the hue,
Faint salmon-yellow, sprigged with rosy bloom,
And drenched, my child, with Lubin's best perfume.
Did you not notice it?   Scent to suit the sprigs;
A perfume for each dress, a bottle per robe;
It is—expensive, but it pleases me,

Amuses me, and look ! it will amuse
" Society " too, the paper and the thing.
Society's a noun and singular,
So *very* singular, I find at times,
But as it likes me, I've no fault with it,
And you're at liberty, Justine, to tell
The indolent reviewers, editors,
Reporters, critics, hangers-on the press
And loungers at stage doors, even " The Bat,"
About the perfume. Quite the newest thing.
Madame—*c'est moi*—has set in fairy freak
A fairy fashion in her own grand way.
So—you may tell them. Now, Justine, make haste.
I shall be late, child. Set those roses higher,
Nearer my shoulder—so. My skin will fire
Later, upon the stage, but now 'tis cold
And gray. Justine, I am not growing old !
'Tis but the worry and the hours you think ?
It soon will pass, you're sure ? I trust so. Higher
Please set those roses. Here's a branch of briar
Bound in with them ! That makes me think, Justine,
How *you're* the briar, *I* the grand red rose.
You the neat Breton maid not long from airs
Of rustic France, your cap, your gown, your shoes,
Your necklace and your braided plaits of brown,
Gaze with the young maid's trick—that looking down.
I—the forced product of a crowded town,

I—born with spangles in my eyes and clash
Of brass within my ears, I—grown to fame
And fortune most illimitable—yes,
I am the rose, the Jacqueminot, and you,
The wild sweet briar, sweetly bound to me
In this great London.   Come, that pleases me,
A pretty parallel, so apposite.
I always had a literary turn,
And yet will write my plays myself and for
Myself.   O *ego, ego, ego!*   Cease—
This wild inchoate talk !   Justine, I go.
The rose has duties that the briar escapes ;
Her velvet heart lies open, and its glow
Must help to warm the world, the world indoors
That has in truth but little taste for briars,
Accounting such but weeds.   All briars but weeds ?
You don't know logic yet.   Well, now I go.
Have coffee on the stroke of twelve—I'll bring
A Cardinal, a Poet—perhaps a King
Home here to supper.   *   *   *   *
  *   *   *   *   *   *   *   *   *

NOVEMBER.

NOVEMBER.

THESE are the days that try us; these the hours
That find, or leave us, cowards—doubters of Heaven,
Sceptics of self, and riddled through with vain
Blind questionings as to Deity. Mute, we scan
The sky, the barren, wan, the drab, dull sky,
And mark it utterly blank. Whereas, a fool,
The flippant fungoid growth of modern mode,
Uncapped, unbelled, unshorn, but still a fool,
Fate at his fingers' ends, and Cause in tow,
Or, wiser, say, the Yorick of his age,
The Touchstone of his period, would forecast
Better than us, the film and foam of rose
That yet may float upon the eastern grays
At dawn to-morrow.
                                    Still, and if we could,
We would not change our gloom for glibness, lose
Our wonder in our faith. We are not worse
Than those in whom the myth was strongest, those
In whom first awe lived longest, those who found
--Dear Pagans—gods in fountain, flood and flower.

Sometimes the old Hellenic base stirs, live,
Within us, and we thrill to branch and beam
When walking where the aureoled autumn sun
Looms golden through the chestnuts. But to-day—
When sodden leaves are merged in melting mire,
And garden-plots lie pilfered, and the vines
Are strings of tangled rigging reft of green,
Crude harps whereon the winter wind shall play
His bitter music—on a day like this,
We, harbouring no Hellenic images, stand
In apathy mute before our window pane,
And muse upon the blankness. Then, O, then,
If ever, should we thank our God for those
Rare spirits who have testified in faith
Of such a world as this, and straight we pray
For such an eye as Wordsworth's, he who saw
System in anarchy, progress in ruin, peace
In devastation. Duty was his star—
May it be ours—this Star the Preacher missed.

THE BALL AND THE STAR.

(AS ONE SPEAKS.)

Do I hold my life in my hand
    . To make or to mar,
        To prize or let·fall,
To round to the perfect ball,
To mould to the matchless star?

Here has rolled to my halting feet,
        From the nursery stair,
        From the children's nest,
A rubber thing that is drest
With a gaudy patchwork air.

Its colours I may not admire;
        Bright red and bright green
        Are not to my taste,
And their vulgar is not effaced
By the line of yellow between.

Still, 'tis a ball, and that's much,
        Made fit to bound,
        Made fit to stay
On a table—that is away
From the edge—or upon the ground,

Even it, a ball, will fall,
        That's nought of a fault,

As I see, in the ball,
But in the putter—in all
That becomes a ball, to vault,

To roll and rebound, how full,
How round it must be!
How smooth, without trace
Of ragged and jagged rough on its face,
To rebound so swiftly, so perfectly!

It does its work well, no doubt.
Ah! yes, but then
It is well made,
Of its work not a whit afraid,
Though only fashioned by men.

Only fashioned by men, I think—
What do I know?
What does it matter?
Upstairs, a more divine clatter,
Hiding, hunting, the children go.

The truant toy has been missed;
With ecstacy—
Mothers know how—
A child, with an innocent brow,
And eyes o'erbrimming with glee,

Will gather to him the ball;
    The vulgar yellow,
    The glaring green,
Will cosily, safely lie between
The pinky fists of the little fellow.

" Wanted," the ball is. Has its place.
    The little hands
    Are quick and kind,
And the little eyes are seldom blind,
'Tis a little child who understands

That the ball has rolled and rolled and rolled
    Far from its home,
    From the nursery stair,
Far from the innocent upper air—
Even a rubber thing will roam.

What does it suffer in roaming? Not it.
    It will return
    Just as it came,
Not a whit broken, marred or lame;
The ball you see, has nothing to learn,

Nothing to spend and nothing to save,
    Nothing to give,
    Except some day

Its round and beautiful life away.
How long ere that be? Might it not live

Forever with care on a shelf somewhere,
        Where pins are not,
        And needles gay,
For ever and ever are out of the way?—
What was the other wandering thought?

Oh! here, this morning on my sleeve,
        Appeared a star,
        With a wonderful law
In its wonderful points, with not a flaw
In its beauty although it fell so far.

It breathed for a moment, then died.
        While I stood at the door
        And counted its rays
It died at the strength of my gaze.
From a snow-star, so much and no more!

Perfect the ball and the star,
        Each in its day,
        Each in its end.
I shall never mend! I shall never mend!
I, imperfect, will go away.

           *   *   *   *   *

Do I hold my life in my hand,
    To make or to mar,
    To prize or let fall,
To round to the matchless ball,
To mould to the radiant star?

THE TREE.

Was there no beauty, then, in barren stem,
   No symmetry in jagged twig and limb,
That slow discarding lustrous diadem
   Lay etched upon the sunset's orange rim?

Were it, too, better never to have been
   A thing leaf-crowned and wholly, freshly fair;
A being all benignant, purely green,
   Sheltered and sheltering, innocent of care?

Strange—that for half the year the tree must go
   Uncrowned, unclad, soul-shivering to the blast,
Each glossy leaf be trodden deep in snow,
   Each acorn to the ground be roughly cast!

Careless of coming frost aloft it looks,
   All confident of many another spring,
O'er dry, brown fields and saddened, silent brooks,
   And woods where not a bird is left to sing.

This the great secret of its grand content,
   This the full meaning of its giant calm,
This the true measure of the reverent
   Straight mien that springtime's sweetest airs embalm.

O, to have been the tree—and not the man!
   To grow in ever wheeling, circling pride,
Conscious of all the noble, gracious plan
   That smiled at Doubt and gave a God to guide!

Think ! to have harboured orange oriole,
   And flaming tanager and chattering jay,
And wise gray sparrow—would not this console
   The weariness born of many a leafless day ?

Since it were known—they come again in five
   Or six months' time of waiting, then to wait,
Even through songless seasons, were to thrive
   On sweet probation, though in sombre state.

Were it not bliss, some melting morn in June,
   To look and see among one's crumpled leaves—
Late to unfold, but deep at heart in tune
   With all of green the young wood interweaves—

A flash of living light, incarnate gem,
   That holds a voice in quivering, ruffled throat,
That hangs, a jewel, on the budding stem,
   That sings a song of Hope—Death's antidote ?

CHRISTMAS.

Who will sing the Christ?
　　Will he who rang his Christmas chimes
　　Of faith and hope in Gospel ray,
　　That pealed along the world's highway,
　　And woke the world to purer times—
　　　　Will he sing the Christ?

Or that new voice which vaguely gives—
　　One day its song for Rome—the next,
　　In soul-destroying strife perplext
　　For England's faith and future lives—
　　　　Shall he sing the Christ?

Or the sweet children in the schools,
　　That hymn their carols hand-in-hand
　　All purely, can they understand
　　The wisdom that must make us fools—
　　　　Can they sing the Christ?

Or yearning priest who to his kind
　　From carven pulpit gives the Word,
　　Or praying mother who has erred,
　　And blindly led her erring blind—
　　　　Have they not sung the Christ?

" Lord ! I of sinners am the chief !"
One, seated by his Christmas fires,
Hearkens the bells from distant spires,
But hangs his head in unbelief—
      He cannot sing the Christ.

Grant to such, Lord, the seeing eye !
Grant as the World grows old and cold,
All hearts Thy beauty may behold.
Grant, lest the souls of sinners die—
      That All may sing the Christ.

THE POET'S SUNDAY.

"You will not go to church?" she said,
    And a soft psalm of sad dissent
    Might in her mien so reverent
        Be easily read.

He broke a branch of lilac-bloom
    That twisted greenly in and out;
    He shook its honey all about
        The morning-room.

"I do not see why I should leave
    So sweet a Sunday thing as this,
    Wet with the dawn's last dewy kiss,
        Love, a reprieve!"

"I may not grant you one," she sighed,
    "I think that you might come; I know
    That if you knew he wished it so—
        The one who died——

"I do know, Dear, and yet alone,
    I fear me, you must go to-day;
    For if I went, I could not stay;
        The monotone·

Of this clear blue intensely fair,
    Would draw me forth from hymn and chant,
    To seek and seal fresh covenant
        With sky and air ;

Those dew-washed grasses keenly green,
    Like freshly-sharpened scimetars,
    That give such tiny fragrant scars,
        Would intervene,

When paler emerald darted down,
    With amethyst and ruby rays,
    That sooner pall than yonder jay's
        Blue coat and brown.

The morning grandeur of this wind!
    Hark! how it blows, and sweeps, and swings
    Across the world on nobler wings
        Than those of tinned

And gilded glories—boxed-up Hope,
    And Charity on cold white planes,
    And Faith—nay, wait, it but remains
        To say, for Pope,

Parson, Revivalist, or Priest,
    (They're very much the same, I find,
    And much like other human-kind,)
        I'll have at least

As good a thinker as you know,
    The dear old drone, whom you admire—
    Child, can it be you never tire,
        And wish to go

Elsewhere? Yet that were foolish too!
    I hold, the small and servile sects
    Are vainly in themselves perplext,
        Teach nothing new.

O in this hurried world to-day
    Some things must go! Men are not now
    What once they were; the lifted brow,
        The serious way,

The rapture and the reverie
    Of prayer and faith and penitence,
    Suppression Spartan of the sense,
        I nowhere see!

I know two witcheries in Life.
     Now one is Love, (mind, only two,)
     This love is love, my love, of you;
          The other, rife

With all its vast Potential grand,
     And benefit to all the race,
     Is love of Nature. Ah! you place
          A startled hand

Upon my arm! Well then, no more.
     I talk, you know, but *all* I say
     I hardly mean; it is my way
          Headlong to pour

Hellenic jargon in your ear,
     Because you never take offence
     But grant a loving audience—
          What is it, Dear?"

For in her cheek the colour dies,
     And on her lip a tremble sues,
     And something like a tear bedews
          Her lovely eyes.

The Poet laughed, and tossed his hair,
    And flung the lilac-branch away.
"You cannot wear that flower to-day;
    Your pallid air

This morning, Dear, requires a bright
    And warmer tone. Ah! where's the rose,
The crimson one, that monthly blows,
    And seeks the light

In your own window?" Up he leaps,
    And down again before she knows,
And fastens quick the glowing rose
    Beneath the deeps

Of rounded chin and rounder throat,
    Upon the soft gray of her gown.—
The Poet's wife in gray or brown
    Long robes that float

Throughout his house is always drest.
    So soothes she with grave gown and glance
His soul's too gay inheritance,
    She gives him rest.

And now the bells have ceased. A calm
   Has smitten all the little town,
   And in the church the folk kneel down,
      They wear the Palm;

They sing the hymns their fathers knew,
   They hear the story told again
   Of sinless Christ and sinful men;
      Some think it true,

And some have never thought at all,
   But all would fain believe the tale,
   If only once from 'neath the vail
      Some light would fall.

    *   *   *   *

The bells have ceased. The Poet lies—
   Dreaming, musing, upon the grass,
   But through his brain no fancies pass,
      No mysteries

Of saint and satyr, gnome and fay,
   Of king, of jester in disguise,
   Of knight and squire in brilliant dyes
      Upon their way.

Have the bells ceased? He thought to write—
　　Perhaps to rhyme, at least to read
　　The modern master-minds, whose creed
　　　　He takes for light.

The bells have ceased, he knows full well;
　　But though he surely cannot care,
　　He seems to hear them everywhere,
　　　　While with the swell,

And rise and fall, there comes at times
　　A strain of far-off singing clear,
　　And strangely, sadly, dimly dear,
　　　　Above the chimes.

　　　*　　*　　*　　*

What was his motive when he rose,
　　Obedient to the inner peal,
　　Could he himself at will reveal,
　　　　In truth disclose?

What e'er it be it carries him,
　　With curious, not unwilling, feet
　　Along the walk and down the street
　　　　Grass-grown and trim.

The open porch is ivied o'er.   *   *   *
    O do we know a stranger thing
    Than village folk that stand and sing,
        And thus adore

The God they cannot understand,
    For What is it they deify,
    And Whom is it they crucify
        Throughout the land?

Yet do we know a better thing
    Than kneeling folk that for an hour
    Forget their trouble and the power
        Of sin's strong King?

The Poet looked, and something crept—
    A certain softness, in his face,
    And for a happy moment's space,
        He gently wept.

There in her corner sits the wife.
    Ah! but her thoughts are hard to keep
    On Shepherd true and wandering sheep,
        And Bread of Life!

Her sorrow she can scarcely hide,
 —That dreaming figure on the grass—
 Nay, what is this has come to pass?
 He's at her side!

" It is the best thing that we know "—
 He breathes as softly in her ear
 As when he told the tale of fear
 In love—" and so

I come to sit with you—'tis right?
 The lilacs lost their lovely bloom
 And all the world was bathed in gloom,
 Yet here 'tis bright."

She cannot speak nor look at him,
 But reaches forth a little hand;
 He takes it, he will understand,
 Her eyes are dim.

           *   *   *   *

" O little wife," the Poet said,
 While round his neck her arms he placed,
 With his own arms about her waist,
 And on her head

Soft kisses rained; (they were at home,
    And both were happier it seemed,
    Than either one had ever dreamed,)
       " Why did I come

And find you in the well-known pew?
    I hardly know, but since I came—
    Contrite, Dear, with a touch of shame—
       I swear to you,

I'll never let you go again
    All lonely as you went to-day;
    And if, sweet child, I cannot pray
       As you are fain

To have me pray, like him who died,
    Your father, earnest in his work
    Of saving souls, I'll never shirk
       In a false pride

The service I can love so well.
    If in this hurried world of ours
    Some things must go; if waning powers
       Seem to rebel

Because there is too much to learn,
    Too much to do, too much to know.
    And so the crowded days o'erflow,
        And round we turn

On turning earth with never a rest—
    At least we'll try to keep a sense
    For holy things and reverence—
        Sweet gift and blest—

For the dear faith our fathers knew,
    For things of virtue, things of praise,
Of good report and pleasant ways,
        The Good, the True."

THE FIRST CHILL.

Did you not think last night that the summer was over?
That gone were the bees and the broom, and that gone
    was the clover,
That dead were the flowers in your delicate basket of
    wire,
That dead were the trailing tongues of the creeper's
    autumnal fire?

Did you not say to me then that a frost must be falling,
Ere we both saw on the terrace your sweet mother
    calling?
Did we not stand there together and gaze at the gray
That frightened the flushing rose from the cheek of the
    dying day?

Together, and yet apart, while *your* roses were paling,
And you grew cold and white, and I too, and all sweet
    speech seemed failing;
If I spoke, I offended, or thought so; so what could
    I do
But be silent, nor risk the chance of further offence
    against you?

Did I not offer, sweetheart, that time when we tarried,
To put on a gossamer bit of a wrap that you carried?
Did you not calmly regard me as one who ignores,
Just turn without word or smile, and so leave me, and
    vanish indoors?

Did we not think in truth that the summer was over,
That gone were the bees and the broom, and that gone
    was the clover?
While you sat with your feet to the fire, I walked till I
    grew
Half-frozen, half hating the world, the climate, myself,
    and—you.

But now what has happened, that after the wintriest
    weather,
The heart of each bird is as light as the tiniest feather?
The sun is as warm and the grass is as green as in
    June,
And we sing with our hearts and lips, like the birds to
    a summer tune.

Sweetheart! Do thou sob no more! If the love were
    at ending,
If the fault and the fever alike were both beyond
    mending,
Then might you weep like the woman of tears that I
    know,
But not when I strain you thus—not, not when I hold
    you so!

What a mistake, love, to think that the summer was
    over!
I fancy I saw a bee, and I'm sure I smelt clover——
Swear to forget, child, the sudden, the menacing chill
That darkened and startled the world and our hearts
    last night on the hill!

HAPPY !

I.

So. You are " happy," she says—this girl-friend of mine !
I'd cry in a minute—how little she knows—
But that I'm afraid—her eyes are quick eyes to divine
The substance beneath all such honeymoon shows—
She is right—you *are* happy. *I* dare
To doubt both your smile and your succulent
　　satisfied air !

II.

" Clarice, but leave me !"—I cried. Then she crept from
　　the cliff,
For I stamped with my foot and I covered my ears.
I was selfish—mad—stung—stabbed—what ! *we* have a tiff ?
We true friends in trouble, true Clarice in tears ?
My Clarice, forgive me ! For men
Have women forgot other women again and again.

III.

Happy! I could not but hear it, long after she spoke.
　　So. Happy—and sitting at home by the fire,
Or, happy—and out for a walk where the rivulet broke
Into foam at *my* feet. where the scent of the brier
Stole sweet on the air—I dream
Together we stroll by the lucent and shimmering
　　stream !

IV.

And now it's all over, you thought, I expect, like a man,
    I'd come—sly—between you, and ruffle your peace;
Write letters—was that it—and weave in anonymous plan
    A snare for the lady, your wife. No. Her lease
    Of your love, Sir, is her's. I dispute
    With no one about you, walk steady and quiet,
        keep mute.

V.

Yet I know you have never so trusted me; feared, have
        you not,
    When the mail was brought in, or put down by
        her plate,
Bent down the next moment with fingers all trembling
        and hot
    To stroke the meek head—or to see, was it straight,
    The writing, or backhand and fierce.
    There is power then in handwriting? God! *I* know
        how it can pierce!

VI.

Then when you have left her alone all a long afternoon,
    I know you have feared to return and to open the
        door;
My voice—did you hear—her form—was it—huddled in
        swoon,

Or low on her knees did she weep and implore?
I know you have pictured the worst;
I feel you have wanted me dead, or living, accursed.

VII.

But then you are *happy*. You told her to tell me, afraid
I might think the reverse—so—cling to the past,
Disturb you in wooing, burst in with my hair out of braid,
Be once more the genius and leave her aghast—
"She's worse than I thought. Go to!
Such women were never, my lover, intended for you."

VIII.

No, no, it is clear they were not. Too earnest by half;
Too earnest? The word's a reproach to your type!
To be earnest at all is a folly. I hear your low laugh,
You smother a smile as my eyelids you wipe.
Yes, at least you did that. My tears!
What sorrow was mine a year back for your eyes
and your ears!

IX.

And yet as I wept on your shoulder, I knew all the while,
Your eyes were not lamps set to guide;
Your lips, not lips moving with pity but curved in a smile,

Such as *she* never sees in a fright at her side,
You are careful, I know. You wear
Always in her presence that satisfied, confident air.

X.

Marriage is sweet, I suppose. You feel she's your
own,
And should you fall ill, she can sit in a chair
Quite near to your bedside, keep up the dim tone
Of pale sickbed sentiment, measure, prepare
Your physic and phials. Your want
Was greater last year in that brier-sweetened,
blossoming haunt!

XI.

Why, then it was art, books and music, the drone-bee
instinct!
Together we weighed worlds, dissected the sun;
Praised Pater, and Darwin, made notes, got our fingers
well inked,
Together wove verses, made many a pun.
We were equals in all things. Your mate
You declared you had found and from sympathy
Love sprang straight.

XII.

But then you grew tired.   Men do—of a woman like me.
　　You were not quite at ease ; my inviolate mind
Was quicker and fresher from study, you hated to see
　　How aptly I quoted—you hated to find
　　Your peer in a woman.   Be just,
　　O my friend, you might leave us that much, spare
　　　　us that jealous thrust !

XIII.

Cold comfort in coins and conchology, yet all the
　　　　while
A *kind* of equivalent.   Women have changed ;
They love, suffer, love again, live on a glance or a smile
　　For a season till fancy has ebbed, glance has ranged,
　　Then they turn to, and study.   Why, see—
　　It was after we parted, I crammed, conquered, took
　　　　my degree !

XIV.

Sweet solace in science for women as well as for men
　　Is part of our high education.   To jilt
May be still your prerogative.   Now, with a stroke of
　　　　the pen,
　　Or a wave of the brush, we blot out the tears
　　　　spilt—

We endure now like you. At times
We marry, like you, and like you, put ourselves
   in our rhymes.

XV.

Already life smacks of an interest in men and in things ;
   The mortar-board's heavy but suited to curls
That grow--recollect, Sir—like mine in close heavy
    brown rings.
My future is safe—*I*—at least, unlike girls
Who die in their longing—I rise
To full height and true measure. I welcome the
   sorrow that tries.

XVI.

I write, Sir, a poem about you. You'll read and you'll
   laugh,
Then curse—lest the wife should but guess it—no
   name,
Even *Clarice* a feigned one, yet matter too faithful by
   half
To your story and mine. Never fear ; your fair fame
In the world is unscathed. You care
More for that than for anything—wives, they may
   suffer and stare.

SEPTEMBER.

I.

Birds that were gray in the green are black in the yellow.
Here where the green remains rocks one little fellow.

Quaker in gray, do you know that the green is going ?
More than that—do you know that the yellow is showing ?

II.

Singer of songs, do you know that your Youth is flying ?
That Age will soon at the lock of your life be prying ?

Lover of life, do you know that the brown is going ?
More than that—do you know that the gray is showing ?

OCTOBER.

Opaque and dry glows the autumn sky with a blue that
    is merged in shining,
No deep rich hue but a pallid blue that is veiled with
    gray as for lining.
And in heart and mart there be need of art to keep a
    gray world from repining.

For rose and gold cometh snow and cold and a leaden
    sky in the morning,
And the huntsman's pink is a lurid link the lonely valleys
    adorning,
And the feet are fleet the bright hearth to greet, with the
    pack the wet ways scorning.

The leaf is here but it grows full sere and it steadily
    mottles and mellows,
And the chestnuts loom through a golden gloom that is
    lit by the maple yellows,
That nest is best that is hardily drest and secure far beyond
    its fellows.

The jewelled ash makes a flame and a flash the while
    that its leaves are thinning,
But a night and a day and the winds shall have sway
    and these same seared leaves sent spinning,
But a rock and a shock and the winds shall mock at the
    wealth they are wildly winning.

While the leaves still cling may the heart still sing though
    the trees in the storm be straining,
Their trunks showing black in the forest track heaped
    high with the frail ferns' raining,
And the song is strong while the tissued throng faint
    not nor wither in waning.

When they shrivel and shrink even gay hearts think of
    the end that is somewhere in waiting,
When the ash consumes with the sumach plumes and
    there be no birds for mating,
And the wet ways met are the death ways set that the
    wanton winds are creating.

7 P. M.

Eyes looking out to the darkness—for what?—not the
   star
That sparkles down there in the distance, or is it a car
With its red light or green at the end of the street that
   she sees?
Pshaw! she's not looking that way at all; all her soul's
   in the trees
That move darkly above her,. and lean to the passionate
   gust
Of the night wind and rain; there is firmness and
   sweetness and trust
In that sweet face of hers. Not the girl nor the woman
   to mind
The cold drops on cheek and on hair, though the last *be*
   will find,
All uncurling and sleek and pushed back from the brows—
   Though is it a lover?
         Who knows?
   I only suppose,
For I do not know her—I caught but her face and her
   eyes,
As I passed in the rain, muffled up in an autumn disguise.
Eager to be with my own by the side of a fire,
My own that count seven every night and never will tire
Of the day's work and doing told lazily round the big
   table,
Where with her knee-pinned seam, sits Mabel, wife Mabel.

Years ago—I was rather a desperate fellow they say.
Perhaps they are right, and perhaps I had but my day
Of loud careless deeds and a louder and more careless
    tongue ;
    But then I met Mabel. " Too young !"
    That was flung
In our faces for months, till I suddenly took for my own
What so clearly was meant for me—why, had she lastly
    not grown
To leap at my coming and fall on my neck ? Lovely,
    too !
This was the wife that I married. Oh ! Pity that you,
My good sir, her father, a dear old man too in your way,
Should have met me with curses and begged of your
    daughter to stay.
Could she stay ? That I asked her, but she with her
    love made wild,
Just turned on her heel, (she too was a wayward child)
    And that was the end of it. Since—
    Why it makes me wince,
When I remember, that only one moment at night,
In a car-flashed glance, did she see that old man alight,
The only time since we were married—Is *she* still there,
- At the door with the rain beating down on her cheeks
    and her hair !
Rain makes one moralize. Now, I should *not* like to
    think

That it is for the lover she waits; not the woman to
    shrink—
I caught that—from anything. Perhaps, if it be not a
    lover
It may be her husband. Will women ever discover
How selfish men are and how little worthy the waiting?
    Yet if Mabel had thought so, relating
    Our happy mating
Would be out of the question. Now we are happy of
    course ;
Our struggle for place and position and money—the source
Of all good and beautiful things one would have for one's
    own—
All the struggle I say, all our troubles are well-nigh flown
Only sometimes I have thought—how cold the wind grows!
Never mind, but one short block more and then for a
    coze—
I fervently hope that the unknown and sweet-faced girl,
She with her eyes on the dark and her hair out of curl,
Has gone in from the cold and the rain—I was going
    to say
    That my wife, with her way,
    —A womanly way—
Might do much—ah ! so much—for an old man at home
    like him,
Her father I mean. I suppose now, my eyes will be dim,
And my walk be a totter, with everything dropping away

Into the echoing past or the echoless future, some day,
And then, why a womanly touch on my shoulder or hair,
Will not be, I grant, a superfluous thing to bear.
But then is not now. For the present, I really believe
That I shook off but yesterday Mabel's small hand from
    my sleeve ;
I was writing, I think—ah ! " Persephone," now I
    remember !
The dullest of tragedies grows in a dull November,
    And I do not write,
    With the easy flight
All-compelling of yore, why, it takes me far longer to
    fill in
One page in these days than a dozen of former distilling,
When the blood (that of youth) was up ever and ever
    enjoying,
And pleasure and mirth ran high with never a cloying.
The wind, what a wind ! Is Mabel, I wonder, peering
Out from her pleasant comfort to watch me steering
My way through the cold dreary mistiness wind and rain ?
It's beating I know, 'gainst her red curtained window pane ;
It's beating directly, I fancy, against another
South window I know, where in summer the roses half
    smother
Its cosy half-length—I stood among them there often.
Will things ever be better ? Who knows ? 'Tis for him
    to soften ;

What we have done we have done ; yet perhaps had we
    tried,
Things had been better ere now and the twelve years'
    pride
Broken down or dissolved, or never suffered to live.
After twelve years it is easy to say, forgive,
    And as hard to say, forget.
    His Mabel ! His pet !
I figure him now by a fire in an easy chair,
But no one to bend over, kissing the whitened hair ;
He was fond of the taste of a pipe ; on the mantleshelf
It used to be kept—can he reach it now himself ?
Ah ! a woman's care ! Now I *should* like to think that
    the girl—
She with her eyes on the dark, with her hair out of curl,
Is waiting and watching, neither for friend nor for lover,
Neither for friend nor for brother, while it darkens
    above her,
But only—ah, Mabel my darling, my loved one—oh !
    rather,
Rather a thousand times, say, for *only her father !*

          *   *   *   *   *

Four steps, now the door—so dark I can hardly find it,
The red blind at last, and Mabel's dear shadow behind it !

THE DYING YEAR.

THE old year dies! Of this be sure,
     The old leaves rot beneath the snow,
     The old skies falter from the blow
Dealt by the heavens that shall endure
     When sky and leaf together go.

And some are glad and some are grieved,
     Much as when some poor mortal dies;
     The first sensation of surprise
Is lost in sobs of his bereaved,
     Or cold relief with dry-dust eyes,

That view his coffin absently,
     And wonder first how much it cost,
     And next, how came his fortune lost,
And how will live his family,
     And how he looked when he was crost.

But tears—no, no—they only surge
     From those who knew him. They were few;
     He had his faults; he seldom knew
The thing to say, condemn, or urge;
     'Tis better he has gone from view.

So neither do we weep—God knows,
 We have but little time for tears!
 A time for hopes, a time for fears,
A time for strife, a time for woes
 We have—but hardly time for tears.

O it were good, and it were sweet,
 If we might weep our fill somewhere,
 In other world, in purer air,
Perhaps in heaven's golden street,
 Perhaps upon its crystal stair!

For "power and leave to weep" shall be
 The golden city's legend dear;
 Though wiped away be every tear,
First for a season shall flow free
 The floods that leave the vision clear!

So if we could we would, Old Year,
 Conjure a tear up when you go,
 And pace in solemn order slow
Behind your gray and cloud-borne bier, .
 Draped with the wan and fluttering snow.

Yet what is it, this year we miss?
    An arbitrary thing, a mark;
    A rapid writing in the dark;
Dead wire, that with a futile hiss
    Strikes back no single answering spark.

There is no year, we dream and say,
    Again, *no year,* we say and dream,
    And dumbly note the frozen stream,
And note the bird on barren spray,
    And note the cold, though bright sunbeam.

We quarrel with the times and hours,
    The year should end—we say—when come
    The last long rolls of March's drum,
And too—we say—with grass and flowers
    Should rise the New Year, like to some

Gay antique goddess, ever young,
    With pallid shoulders touched with rose,
    Firm waist that mystic zones enclose,
White feet from violets shyly sprung,
    Her raiment—that the high gods chose.

And yet the poet, born to preach
    With yearning for his human kind,
    His verse but sermon undefined,
Will fail in what he means to teach,
    If he proclaim not, high designed,

The Old Year dies! It is enough!
    And he has won, for eyes grow dim
    As passeth slow his pageant grim,
And many a hand both fair and rough
    Shall wipe away a tear for him—

For him, and for the wasted hours,
    The sinful days, the moments weak,
    The words we did or did not speak,
The weeds that crowded out our flowers,
    The blessings that we did not seek.

DECEMBER.

I long for a noble mood. I long to rise,
Like those large rolling clouds of ashen pink
That deepen into purple, over strife
And small mechanic doings. How superb
That landscape in the sky to which I walk,
And gain at will a spacious colour-world,
In which my finer self may feel no fear!
The distance far between that goal and me
Seems lightly bridged; breathless, I win that goal—
The shores of purple and the seas of gold.
Below, how flat the still small earth—a sphere
That only the leaden soul takes solace in!
The long pine stretches, barred in sombre black,
Cross at right-angles fields that are gray with snow—
Not white, but gray, for all the colours is here,
Colour—a new sacrament—melted gems,
The hearts of all water-lilies, the tips of their wings—
Young angels', plumed in topaz, garnet, rose—
The dazzling diamond white, the white of pearl.
How poor a place the little dark world appears,
Seen from this gold-cloud region, basoned in fire!
Only a step away, and nothing is seen
Of the homes, huts, churches, palaces it bears
Upon its dry brown bosom. There remains
But the masterful violet sea, that angrily
This moment somewhere gnashes its yellow teeth

Against a lonely reef. What's most like God
In the universe, if not this same strong sea,
Encircling, clasping, bearing up the world,
Blessing it with soft caresses, then, for faults,
Chiding in God-like surges of wrath and storm ?
But the ocean of cloud is placid, and the shores,
Rolled up in their amethyst bulk towards the stars,
Fade noiselessly from pearl to purple dark.
The shades fall even here. Here—not exempt
From death and darkness even these shining airs—
The night comes swifter on than when on earth.
The fringes of faintest azure, where the bars
Of paler cloud are fading into gray,
Are dulled and blotted out. Opaque has grown
The molten in one moment; fleecy pale
And ghastly all the purple—lonely then,
And awed to horror of those glacial peaks,
I bridge the vaporous barrier once again,
And tread the despisèd earth. Then how too dear
Doth the rude, common light of earth appear—
That of a street lamp, burning far, but clear !
The sign of human life, of human love,
Of habitation sweet, of common joys
And common plans, though precious, yet not prized,
Till in a moment's fancy I had lost them.

THE RIME OF THE *GRAY CITIE.*

I.

From firelight to starlight,
(And northward flies a flame)
It streameth high to the Polar sky,
And a pageant doth proclaim ;
While the *Gray Citie* that is crowned of the cold,
Hath need of a singer proud and bold.

II.

She sigheth, she lieth
Prone on her couch of snow,
She feels the beat of the stranger feet
That through her ways o'erflow,
And her soul from the sordid things of sense
Awakes to a present nobler tense.

III.

She thinketh, she dreameth,
She broodeth on a throng
Of voices great that might dedicate
To her worthily their song,
But she faileth to find, doth the *Gray Citie*,
The while that she holdeth revelry

IV.

In firelight, in starlight,
In dreaming or at day,
The voice, the song that to her may belong
And illuminate her way,
And speak to her sisters over seas,
Of her stately streets and her crowded quays.

V.

She stoopeth, back loopeth
(The better she may see)
Her pine-dark hair from her forehead fair,
Thus watching waiteth she;
And then that the better she may hear,
She turns to the air her listening ear.

VI.

The northward, the southward,
She scans with vision rare,
But the north-song star a cloud doth mar,
Laughs the south in its song so fair,
And no song lives in the red sunset,
And the dawn declares no singer yet.

VII.

She stayeth, delayeth,
For fear that she may miss
A half-blown sigh, or a word, or a cry,
Or a string-swept, heart-flung kiss;
But she waiteth in vain for a minstrel bold,
And the sigh that is wafted upon the cold
From her own heart comes I wis.

VIII.

She rises, she hearkens
To the roar of a hundred guns,
She opens her eyes on a light that vies
With the glare of a thousand suns,
And a million arrows overhead
To the Polar sky stream blue and red.

IX.

To northward from southward
The gay processions wind,
To mount from quay of the *Gray Citie*,
And she maketh up her mind
To-night by herself in her own clear tongue
Shall now or never her song be sung.

X.

"O hear me! Draw near me!"
She towereth where she stands,
Her voice rings loud to the careless crowd,
She spreadeth forth her hands,
On her brow the crystal ice crown gleams,
At her feet the frozen river dreams.

XI.

"O hear me! Draw near me!
And rest from revelry!
The silken mask and the flowing flask,
The varied garb of glee,
The shining skate and the swift snowshoe,
Lay down with the tasselled tuque of blue,

XII.

While welcome, twice welcome,
Thrice with my strongest call
A welcome loud from Mount Royal proud
Do I bid you one and all,
And bid you too in my pleasures share,
My winter glories of sky and air.

XIII.

From flowerlight to firelight,
    (And northward flies a flame),
O first to you is a greeting due,
        You from the south who came,
Leaving your golden orange trees,
Your sweet acacia scented breeze!

XIV.

From coast-land to inland,
    Leaving the fresh salt spray,
There sat at my feast to-day from the east
    Keepers of holiday;
My people all (thus the *Gray Citie*)
Do bid you a welcome fair and free.

XV.

And leaving the heaving
    Green of the prairie wave,
A jovial guest, came you from the west,
    Singing a lusty stave,
The pallor perished, the white hands brown,
With glory of health for your manhood's crown.

XVI.

You others, my brothers,
Remember as you dash
Down the steep white hill while your hearts stand still
And the sharp wind stings like a lash,
My peace, my perils, my foes, my fears,
Two hundred and forty-seven years

XVII.

I count, I remember,
Since one soft summer night,
An altar green was strangely seen
Festooned with fireflies bright,
And the forest tall stood dark above
The form of the martial *Maisonneuve*.

XVIII.

And dreaming, in seeming,
I bow to the saintly *Mance ;*
The face I see of the fair *Peltrie*
As she stands in a heavenly trance;
And the gentle Marguerite *Bourgeoys*,

Charming the sullen Iroquois
            From the maze of his savage dance,
I see by the side of those pioneers,
The Frenchmen who gave their blood, their tears
            For the flag and faith of France!

XIX.

Thus learning, discerning
            Lessons the Past has taught,
You dare not despise the heroes I prize,
            Nor the later lives that brought
The merchant-ships to my harbour gay,
And cut through my cold limestone their way.

XX.

Disdaining complaining,
            The New World bent to their power,
As had done the Old, nor failed to unfold
            The pod, the plant, the flower,
While the beaver stared and stared in vain,
And the Red man's heart nigh broke in twain.

XXI.

And packing and filling
The house and cellar and bin,
My people dare love the icy air,
And they love the silver din
Of the fur-trapt sleighs, nor do they disdain
The loveliness of the frosted pane
When the fire is red within."

XXII.

She pauses, the *Citie;*
Then to her own she saith,
" Look ye agree in your revelry
To revere both pain and death;
And forget not the poor in their poverty,
So shall ye bless yourselves and me."

XXIII.

From firelight to starlight,
To the north there darts a flame,
It streameth high to the Polar sky
And a pageant doth proclaim.
Unchecked once more is the revelry
In the streets and paths of the *Gray Citie.*

VILLANELLE.

A Girl's idea of Greece.
    Huge honeycombs, rich dates,
Goats and the Golden Fleece;

Gods pretty much of a piece,
    Jumbled up with the Fatês,
(A girl's idea of Greece!)

Ganymede Saturn's niece,
    Mercury given to skates,
Goats and the Golden Fleece:

Drapery *minus* a crease,
    Dryads polishing plates,
A *girl's* idea of Greece!

Hush! Bid the clatter cease!
    Lest while the novice prates
Of Goats and the Golden Fleece,

The halls of Girton release
    The maid who matriculates.
" A girl's idea of Greece!
    Goats and the Golden Fleece!!!"

VILLANELLE.

Sprung from a sword-sheath fit for Mars,
     Straight and sharp, of a gay glad green,
My jonquil lifts its yellow stars.

Barter, would I, for the dross of the Czars,
     These golden flowers and buds fifteen,
Sprung from a sword-sheath fit for Mars?

Barter, would you, these scimitars,
     Among which lit by their light so keen
My jonquil lifts its yellow stars?

No, for the breast may burst its bars,
     The heart its shell, at sight of the sheen
Sprung from a sword-sheath fit for Mars:

Miles away from the mad earth's jars,
     Beneath a leafy and shining screen,
My jonquil lifts its yellow stars.

And I—self-scathèd with mortal scars,
I weep, when I see, in its radiant mien,
Sprung from a sword-sheath fit for Mars
My jonquil lift its yellow stars.

FRAGMENT.

A yellow moon shines
    On the inturned breast of Nuphar,
    She the golden river lily;
    On the wedding ring of the bride
    Glowing with love, adoring in happy pride;
On the hair above the brows of innocent childhood;
On the rustling corn far away in a meadow;
On the gleaming coin which fell in the shadow;
On the cloth of gold of a king;
On the tender midnight blossoming
Of briar-bud to rose.

A wan white moon shines
    On a lily they took from the river,
    Larger and whiter than all the rest.
    Trampled and soiled is its delicate breast.
    On the satin and snowy robe
She will wear on the morrow,
Who will loathe to be called a wife;
What sorrow is like to her sorrow?
On the stiffening, straggling gray-white locks
Of the old man murdered;
On the pale ones who long for bread;
On the silver snake round the arm of a woman
Who longs in her soul to be dead;
On the shroud of a young new mother and babe;
On the shedding of blossoms and tears
O'er the mound and the marble.

OF YE HEARTE'S DESIRE.

Wythe some it is shippes and golde;
　　Wythe some it is palaces faire;
Wythe some it is blossoms that folde
　　Theire beautie away fromme the aire;
Wythe some it is castles in Spaine,
　　That tower through a rosie cloude;
Wythe some it is visions of paine
　　That compass them here like a shroud.

Wythe others 'tis feasting and fun,
　　The thyng they call "lyfe," no doubt;
Wythe some it is fame well-done
　　And garnished with puffes about;
Wythe some it is places highe;
　　Wythe some it is stockes and shares;
Wythe others 'tis kites to flie;
　　Wythe some it is fancie faires.

Wythe some it is grace to walk
　　Through lyfe aright to the grave;
Wythe some it is yearning to talk
　　Wythe the friend beyond the wave;
Wythe some 'tis to make new friends,
　　Wythe others to keep but one;
Wythe some 'tis to make both ends
　　Meet as they never have done.

None of these wyshes are myne.
Lovers who guess my plight,
Reading between each lyne
Lo, ye have guessed aright!
Only my hearte's desire—
To feel that my love forgives,
That his hearte will never tire ·
Of loving me while he lives!

A PLEA.

For the Idle Singers of an Empty Day.

Not by us the seed
   Sown—we only tend it;
Not by us the gift
   Bought—we only send it;
Not by us the flowers
   Plucked—we only fling them;
Not our own the songs,
   But the way we sing them.

Though all blossoms grew
   Cheap—we still should miss them;
Though some gifts appear
   Poor—we often kiss them;
Though the seeds may look
   Small—we cannot spare them;
Though our songs be slight,
   Shall the world not share them?

Now should Fate be kind,
   Cause us to inherit
Sweet access of Fame,
   Based on others' merit,
Hear us now confess,
   As to-day we bring them,
Not our own the songs,
   But the way we sing them.

NIAGARA IN WINTER.

Nor similes nor metaphors avail!
All imagery vanishes, device
Dies in thy presence, wondrous dream of ice!
Ice-bound I stand, my face is pinched and pale,
Before such awful majesty I fail,
Sink low on this snow-lichened slab of gneiss,
Shut out the gleaming mass that can entice,
Enchain, enchant, but in whose light I quail.

While I from under frozen lashes peer,
My thoughts fly back and take a homeward course.
How dear to dwell in sweet placidity,
Instead of these colossal crystals, see
The slender icicles of some fairy " force,"
And break the film upon an English mere!

SONNETS: TO THE GOD OPPORTUNITY.

I.

Strange, that no idol hath been roughly wrought,
Or fairly carven, bearing on its base
A name so potent! Strange, no ancient race,
Workers in whitest Parian, ever sought
To reproduce thy beauty, slyly fraught
With vast suggestion! Strange, thou could'st not brace
The dull Assyrian, did'st not tempt from chase,
Trophy and battle, the sons of literal thought!

We who are tired of gods must yet to thee
Render allegiance. Chance and Love are blind,
And Cause is soulless, Art is deaf and vain,
All unavailing looms the God of Pain.
Disclaiming these, we choose with prescient mind,
The unknown God of Opportunity.

II.

Tired of all other gods are we, and fain
To serve thee for a season; seem'st to nod,
A sleek slim shape, half demon, half a god,
Thy sex unguessed at, eyes that hold a grain
Of maniac cunning, piercing through the sane
Strong gaze of Deity, around a rod
Thy snaky fingers clasped, while near thee plod
The petty things who follow in thy train.

These are Ambition, Circumstance, and Will.
For gods they once were taken by some rule
Forgotten, now with pallid purpose hurled
Down from unstable thrones. Supreme and still,
Thou reign'st, thy rod the lever of the world,
Fortune, thy favourite; Failure, thy poor fool!

MARCH.

With outstretched whirring wings of vandyked jet,
Two crows one day o'er house and pavement pass'd.
Swift silhouettes limned against the blue, they glass'd
Smooth beak and ebon feather in the wet
Of gaping pool and gutter, while, beset
By nestward longing, high their hoarse cry cast
In the face of fickle sun and treacherous blast,
Till all the City smelt the violet.

Then through that City quick the news did run.
Great wheels were slacken'd; belts were stopped in mill,
And fires in forges. Long ere set of sun
Dazed men, pale women sought the open hill—
They throng'd the streets. They caught the clarion cry—
" Spring has come back—trust Spring to never die !"

APRIL.

While others hug the fire, I gladly go,
Blown along beneath April skies to one broad path
That winds away from the town and drops below
A rude plank bridge, to glades that soon shall glow
With violets velvet sheathèd, op'd full rath.

April—the opal month of all the year,
With pearly skies, and blue, and sudden snows—
The opal April of my thought is here,
And I am happy when a star doth peer
From the brown bed of leaves wherein it grows.

I would not touch one downy drooping bud !
The fingers of the wind, alone have power
To give such, life, and soon its peers shall stud
The greening bank that now is caking mud.
I go, return, and wait that magic hour.

The eager children throng about the glade,
They do not know the signs, they falter—doubt
There will be flowers, mistrust the cooling shade
That meets them on the wood's edge, note the fray'd,
Crisp curl'd last winter's leaves the wind still rout.

Indeed, it asks for faith, when all the road
Is furrow'd deep in slowly drying ruts,
And farmers gently urge with sparing goad
Their morning teams, conscious of pressing load,
And squirrels count their yet full store of nuts,

And frosty films on tree and sward are cast,
And rivulets run cold, nor yet too free,
And the old grass is sodden, lump'd and mass'd
On either side the fence, while a March blast
Blows April's trumpeter in triumphant key.

Afar stretch fields exceeding grey and wan,
Of sterile stubble; here are flying leaves,
And clouds of dust the wide highway upon.
It seems some mid-October morn; all gone
The splendour of the gay autumnal sheaves,

And only left, the longing for the snow
To veil defect and compensate for loss.
But not a blossom ever seeks to blow
Until the time be ripe. Let rains but flow,
And stumps shall cushion'd be with emerald moss,

And every bank shall wear a coronet
Of azure stars and yellow bells; pale plumes
Of slow uncurling green be rootwise set,
And higher, where the forest parapet
Its fringe of faint new foliage assumes.

O! I have felt the high poetic mood
While lingering there, far from the troubled ways
Of duty and desire; have lov'd to brood
For hours in the open air—my faith, my food—
Till seemed to cling around my brow the bays!

And I have felt, too, like the vagabond,
Who knows no duty, has but one desire—
To keep the peace with Nature; who, beyond
All envy, sleeps beside some cool clear pond
And sees each morn the flaming sunrise fire

Bleak hill and budding forest—I would give
Much, in such moods, to drop the life I lead,
All ties, all dear expectances and live
As carelessly as that poor fugitive
Of all demands which now I daily heed.

Must heed—for dreaming is not doing. Base,
Base should I be to dream my days to death
In this sequester'd glade, where shadows chase
A golden phantom. To each man his place—
He who neglects his, curses with latest breath

The trend and disposition of his life,
For spells, dew-laden, odorous, warm and soft,
Like these sweet April omens, purely rife
With soothing promise of an end to strife,
Are dangerous. No more then, high aloft,

I lift ecstatic eyes to sheer bright blue,
Or seek the curlèd cup beneath my foot.
I wander homeward, longed for by the few
Who love me, loving, too, the work I do—
See—I have brought them one arbutus root!

OF LOVE IN DANGER.

Out—out—out—and away, away,
    Far away from the sheltering bay,
    With the houses hanging out of the town,
    And the shoeless children at their play
    Happy and hearty and blithe and brown;
    Far away from the daisied down
    That crowns the cliff with a vagrant fine,
    The dashing vagabond columbine;
    Far away, (and I feel no twinge)
    From its scarlet bright familiar fringe;
    Till the houses and cliff are faded quite.
    Only a cottage, small and white,
    Left, as I turn my head to the right,
    Mark it there in the evening light;
    So I drift away from the bay,
            Away, away.

    What do you do out so far?
    Look! already the evening star
    Rises over your beautiful bay;
    Already the children upon the sand,
    Grow tired of glee and tired of play,
    Are clustered in a sleepy band.
    Look! at the window a mother's hand,
    And voices calling "Come in!" Come back!

What will you do when the shadows black
O'ertake you on your seaward tack?
Look! There will be no moon to-night,
And it is not far, not far from the sea;
Drenched you will be,
Do you not hear
Faint but clear,
The mothers' voices calling?

Out—out—out—and away, away,
Further away from the sheltered bay!
I have no fear of the amber floor,
My boat is of amber—I have no oar,
No rudder have I, but I have a sail—
See! when I left it was linen pale,
Now it is fixed to a golden mast,
And silken and yellow it flies full fast!
Smooth are the waters and calm the air,
A great gold light glows everywhere,
So have I seen a sunset rare,
Gild like the mythic god of old
My little town so white and cold,
The little town that is far behind
The silken sail that flies on the wind.
So I drift away from the bay,
              Away, away!

Hist !   For I'd help you yet.
Out of the waves and the wet,
Out of the gathering black,
Here is my voice to say,
While it is light come back !
Drowned you will be ;
Do you not see
There to the right
The open sea ?
Here is my hand to save
From wave upon wave,
From grave upon grave,
And blackness surely descending.
If it were not so dark !
If by some light I might mark
If your journey be ending !
No.   There it is about you,
All the hurry and flash,
And the whirl and the crash
Of the storm about you !
God !   I would help you yet !
Out of the waves and the wet,
Out of the wind and the waves,
Out of the gathering black,
And the gathering graves——

OF LOVE IN REPROOF.

I thought that Life was worth the living,
I thought that Love was worth the giving.

Sweet, do you wonder how I know
What you knew doubtless years ago,

That Life is made up of follies and vices,
And Love *pour passer le temps* suffices?

For though you are young, so young, you go
To the play or ball in a boddice low,

And your hair still curls in a childish way,
And you laugh and sing and jest all day.

Yet are you older far than me;
You are not young as a woman should be

In maiden lore of down-dropt eyes;
Nor would your cheeks pale in a pure surprise

Were I to tell you a tender tale,
Though mine would flush and my voice would fail,

O Sweet, if ever I tried to speak
The passion that makes us both fierce and weak.

It is left me to think what a woman might be,
Had she your eyes, your laugh of glee,

Your hair too—spirals of glossy brown,
I remember the day you took it down——

With just this difference—hear me, Sweet,
Am I hard who yesterday knelt at your feet?—

Her mind should be pure and her heart be young,
With trust in her eyes and truth on her tongue.

Once will I crush your hands in mine,
(I had thought my mother's ring not too fine

For the dear third finger, but back, my pearl,
You were meant for a purer if plainer girl!)

And once will I kiss you, you'll let me, I know,
(And that is bitter) before I go.

What! you move away! Well, perhaps it is best;
Your lips are not made to make men rest.

www.ingramcontent.com/pod-product-compliance
Lightning Source LLC
Chambersburg PA
CBHW020608030726
47497CB00007B/2132